Beginner's Luck

M.J.Furtek

Website: https://mjfurtek.com/

Twitter: @MJFurtek

Email: info@mjfurtek.com

To Mum, for always pushing me to create.

And to Scott, I hope I made a tiny change.

1

Cat And Mouse

The Watcher's eyes panned across the panes of glass, following the figure, measuring the movements. From one to the next, gliding in a smooth motion, tracking every step, the rhythm steady enough to draw the envy of a metronome.

The time was nearing, and the Watcher could feel it. The senses were heightened, the focus narrowed, and the breeze tingling the skin, making the hairs stand on end.
The breathing – steady.
Calm.

The light was low, but it was as low as it was going to get. The crimson backdrop raged a deep burn, painting some things a flattering colour, while distorting others. An uneven spread of luminosity, unfairly distributed to all things below, as with all things. Such was life.
Still surveying, eyes scanning from one window to the next, they stopped upon a pane – a pane which was different. Framing a cherry blossom tree at its centre, leaves dancing around and filling the edges, it was picturesque and almost perfect; perfect except for one thing – the figure wasn't in it.

The pane was empty, and when the Watcher's eyes tracked back to the previous section, that too, was now void of any silhouette.

The eyes widened as quickly as the heart quickened and began to jump from one section to the next, no longer in the smooth, controlled, rhythmic flow that was in place moments ago. The eyes now darted around in untrained fashion, the heart-rate in a mess, thoughts of worst-case scenarios flashed into the Watcher's mind.
Calm gave way to panic.

A long time had passed since last experiencing this sensation – as far back as the early days of training. A period of trial and error, learning from mistakes, and stamping out those little lapses of concentration. A time when refining instant assessments and making decisions as near-perfect as possible were a must. But... there were always external, uncontrollable variables that could creep in at any point. But not at this point, not now. It had barely begun, yet the figure had suddenly back-tracked. *Could it be random?* Maybe. *Could they know something?* No, impossible. The Watcher banished the paranoia instantly, before it reinforced the panic. Procedure had to be remembered; remember RAM: *regain control, assess, move forward.*

Outside, and into the forest.

Stepping between the trees, weaving and swaying in and out, as the gaps between them narrowed. The sun flashed and flickered through when it could, a strobe of light filtering its way through the cracks. The smell of pine wafted up from below, accentuated by the moisture rising from the damp ground. On any other day it would have been a combination worth sitting and enjoying.
But not today.

As the trees parted, the figure flashed back into view, standing still, looking out through a small clearing, just enjoying the view before moving on again, strolling along the path. It had been random after all – a last minute change of mind to walk through the woods. The Watcher slowed back to a walking pace, matching that of the figure in front. Cat and mouse resumed, with the figure none the wiser.

It rarely ever was.

They continued on through the woodland at a leisurely tempo. Just two walkers, getting some exercise and fresh air. That's how it would appear to most. However, one of the walkers knew something different from the other – they knew where this walk was going, and more importantly, how it would end. With the figure back in sight, and false alarm over, it was back to business. Composure regained; it was time.

This had to happen, and happen now.

She couldn't let her target escape.

&

2

Finding That Balance

The air was fresher and even crisper than she remembered. After all, it had been a long time. The faint recollections all but existed in faded memories, some so distant that she sometimes questioned whether they were real.
For the sake of nostalgia, she told herself they were.

The skyline, however, left her in no doubt. That was one thing she was sure about, and had always remembered so vividly. It dared to show flashes and mixtures of colour that other skies wouldn't even dream of, let alone attempt. The stuff of envy.

Iceland had been Hildur's home as a child, but her life had led her away a long time ago, on a different path from most. This was her first time returning, in circumstances she wouldn't have believed back then, even in the wildest of fairy tales told to children. And yet, here she was.
The target left the edge of the wooded area, and made for the large building across the way. The University, a metallic structure, round and smooth, somehow kept its architecture from clashing with the surrounding nature. Hildur couldn't

help but give credit to the architect. She scanned the now larger open area for any onlookers, found none, and walked on.

It wasn't quite how she remembered her homeland, but old memories rarely matched reality; time tended to alter and blur them like water running down a painting, the finer details hard to grasp. Taking in the surroundings as she walked through them, she waited for something to come; a more definitive memory, or a feeling for the place. But nothing. Maybe those things took time.

Hildur continued to follow, holding back but keeping within distance – finding that balance. This was second nature to her now, intrinsically ingrained through the years. To see, and not be seen.

A pair of late-night joggers ambled past her at a social pace, deep in conversation. The talking far exceeded the movement. Both were fully dressed for the occasion: brand-new top-of-the-range running gear and AirPods at the ready. It was more of a fashion contest than a running one. They barely registered Hildur and went on by, before disappearing down the path.

The target entered the building, waving some form of ID over a scanner, either a stolen card or a decent forgery. Either way, it didn't belong to them. From stationary, Hildur accelerated like a bullet, and covered the remaining distance to the door before it had time to swing even halfway shut. There was only going to be one winner.

She eased inside, and stood in the hallway, listening. The faint patter of footsteps echoed around the corner, muffled by a sensible choice of footwear. A smart choice in the present circumstances, but it would soon count for nothing.

Hildur summoned the map of the building in her head, going through all possible routes one last time. She had committed the layout to memory when planning, using physical anchoring techniques to help memorise and solidify the imagery. She had initially looked over the layout while walking through a forest, and was now recalling it in another, helping the neurological pathways fire to freedom. The result: a picture so clear that she might as well have been holding the original in front of her. She had her trainer to thank for that. Atli had always insisted on conditioning the mind as much as the body, if not more. It was times like this that proved he was right.

Hildur rounded the corner, and sighted her target approaching the far end of the hallway. She stood, and steeled herself one last time before advancing – before completing what she had been sent to do. After all this time, she was back here, walking the same ground. Many things had happened since, some she cared to recall, others she didn't. Some she could never let go of, even if she wanted to.

She never thought she would return in these circumstances, and she never would have believed them herself, were it not for having the sun's crepuscular rays breaking through the clouds and warming her face, inhaling the freshest of air, and being in the presence of a person, whom she was about to kill.

Yes, things were certainly different now.

3

Dealer's Choice

After following the first few turns, Hildur found herself standing in a larger opening. The target had advanced along the next corridor and was momentarily out of sight. Hildur paused a few beats, scanning, listening. Empty and quiet.

The place was closed for the summer, with only a skeleton staff around. She moved forward through the room, past a jet-black Steinway grand piano in its centre – a true finishing piece to any room in the soon to be killers' eyes. She would have given anything to sit and play a few notes, perhaps something in the key of E minor – a personal favourite fitting for the occasion. It would have to wait for another time. She moved on through the silence, after her prey.

Hildur entered the last long stretch and readied herself, hands in pockets, gaze fixed straight ahead. She felt a small sense of gratitude at not having to face any obstacles to this point, which proved to be too early, as one came out of a side door, headed in her direction, in the form of a staff member.

She didn't break stride. She kept her gaze straight ahead on her destination. Focused, and ready to return a greeting if needed. If any questions were asked, her greeting would become less jovial, and the level of his curiosity would determine whether the body count would rise. After all, there was only so much she could say about her reason for being there before tripping on details. It was almost always a fifty-fifty chance of someone interacting in some way, sometimes a physical greeting of a nod or smile, sometimes verbal.

On this occasion, it turned out to be both. The man shot a smile, accompanied with a friendly *"Hello"*. She returned them in identical fashion, before re-focusing on the door, and walked past at the same pace, never slowing to invite a potential conversation. The response and look were enough to be friendly, but nothing too memorable. A neutral response, right down the middle. The only thing that mattered – completely forgettable.

That was a small perk of being physically unassuming – people didn't assume. And in this line of work, it was a blessing in disguise. Mixed with a little acting here and there if needed, and maybe even a smile for good measure, she was as good as invisible.
Especially with men – they were the weakest when it came to this.
None would believe what she was capable of, even if she told them. They would laugh it off. But she could – and had – snatched the life from a man in under ten seconds. The body hadn't come to rest on the floor before she was gone and out of the door.
Speed kills.

Small encounter dealt with, she closed in. She paused, listened, then slowly entered. While most would have surroundings slowly drip-fed through several movements of the head, clunky and slow, Hildur's scan was smooth and fluid. Conditioning had taught her to pick up everything in an instant snapshot, using peripheral vision to its full potential. A complete screenshot, straight to her brain.

The image revealed the room in its entirety, which she processed and dissected in under a second. Electrical equipment scattered throughout; an amalgam of computers, monitors and hard drives, humming and flashing away. The IT department.

Hildur's target was uploading malware via a USB to the mainframe computer – a physical cyber-attack, the quickest and most efficient. Afterwards, all it would take was for someone to open the file, and the malicious code would run riot across the network and its computers undetected. Once in, the attacker could see all. More importantly than the remote viewing, they could remote control, and send on the malicious code via innocent emails to anyone they chose: banks, government departments, the national cyber defence team. In essence – dealer's choice.

Access could be gained remotely, but it would be slower. And why bother when someone else can do it for you at a click of a button? Sometimes the simplest way was the best.

The hacker worked for a group going by the name of Fenrir; a mythical and tyrannical beast that did the bidding of its father, Loki.

How cute, Hildur thought.

Hildur watched as they inserted the drives, shifted items from one place to another, more plugging and unplugging. Hildur didn't understand the intricacies of hacking; it wasn't her area of expertise.

That, was about to come up.

In a cyber battle, the target could outwit Hildur every day of the week. Unfortunately for them, computing wouldn't get them out of this situation. This about to be physical warfare.

Hildur's domain.

Hildur stood around average height, and didn't have the kind of physique that would turn heads or threaten. Her clothing was never too tight, so as to not give away the strength she hid. Underneath was pure, toned muscle. Not bulky enough to ever slow her down or affect her stamina, but sufficient enough to beat most in physical contests.

Hildur had once outlasted all but one of the other trainees at the organisation on an hour-long rock-climbing exercise on Stetinden mountain in Norway, and was the only one of them to complete a route on Flatanger, in Hanshelleren Cave. Not many can say to have climbed any route there, let alone one of the more challenging ones. Her fellow trainees were too hulking and cumbersome to even come close. They spent too much time packed into gyms, shaping and sculpting. Getting the '*look*'. But it wasn't practical, and she showed them just that when they sparred, leaving them on their backs, using their own weight against them.
She couldn't remember any of them ever commenting on her size again after that.

With the target still fully engrossed in what they were doing, they were also offering their back to Hildur. Now was as good a time as any. She edged closer, reducing the gap. With just two metres separating them, Hildur withdrew the syringe, raised it to neck height, and applied the smallest of pressure to feed the fluid to the end of the needle. Primed and ready.
With no reaction from the target, Hildur moved in for the strike.

4

TESS, For Short

Hildur exited the same way she had entered. She stepped out into what was left of the day and took deep a breath. And then another. Her heart rate still hadn't settled; she thought it would have by now. She continued inhaling deeply, trying to get it back to something resembling normal. She closed her eyes and narrowed her focus on just that. The breaths were starting to become slower, and less erratic. Her hands still tremored in small twitches, she clenched to suppress them. She opened her eyes again and started to walk.

The fresh air was welcome, as were the last few rays of sunlight breaking through the ever-growing and gathering clouds, before that particular fight was done for the day and darkness had its inevitable win. The sun would soon be back with a vengeance.

Midnight in an Icelandic summer wasn't an ideal time to try to be surreptitious, with almost 24 hours of daylight provided by the elements at that time of year. It had its strengths and weaknesses, depending on timing. This had been identified as a fitting time to utilise the elements, mainly by her employer, although she agreed with them. It was always best to agree with them.

Hildur was part of an organisation that was as invisible as it was deadly, matching efficiency with anonymity in a perfect balance. A lethal combination. Some believed it existed, while others thought it nothing more than legend; but all had spoken its name.

The moniker would vary depending on who spoke about them, but the fear remained consistent. Sometimes known as 'Norse Draugr' – North Ghosts – on account of never being seen, and other times simply as 'Nordic Morðingjar' – Northern Killers. The most commonly used, and self-appropriated by the organisation itself, was 'The Elite Scandanavian Syndicate' – or TESS, for short.

It operated out of the Nordic territories, and its influence usually stayed within those confines. While crime existed in the Nordic countries, it was low-level petty crime, or, at worst, gangs. TESS existed on a level above that, partly from necessity, and partly from opportunity; as long as it stayed in its zone and didn't tread outside of it, the organisation was the all-seeing and all-saying power. TESS decided what went, and what didn't.

It dealt with problems that needed fixing, either on its own account or for those who paid for its services. Sometimes it dealt with political matters, using influence and cunning; other times, cold-blooded assassinations provided by a highly-skilled coterie of killers at their disposal. Similar to that of a storm, sometimes with little or no warning, TESS destroyed all in their path. The people above Hildur planned and chose the targets, and sent people like her as the destroyers. They were the calm before the storm, the gentle burgeoning breeze; Hildur was the fully-formed hurricane.

After many years of training and tackling smaller objectives, this was her first full international mission, one which she needed to now execute with a successful escape.

She carried out customary scans of the road and surroundings, giving any potential dangers a chance to make themselves known.
None wanted to.
With the coast clear, she headed for something that had caught her eye, a pair of symmetrical church spires, sitting against the backdrop of the fading sky, black on dark blue, almost at one with each other.
A good place to let the nerves settle.

Hildur let a car go past, then stepped onto the road, still looking at the gothic church. She wasn't one for praying, but liked the peace and serenity they had to offer. Everything else that went on inside was up for debate.

She continued to wonder why her heart-rate still hadn't settled, and why her hands still shook at her sides. It was over and dealt with, as she had seen fit.

She wondered if she could have executed the mission differently, if she had covered her tracks sufficiently. Possible scenarios ran themselves ragged in her calculation, so she put a stop to them.

And then she wondered why she was being blinded by lights to her right, as the whole of the left side of her body met with the road, and for the first time in two days, Iceland went dark.

5

Plain White Ceiling

Beep...
Muffled voices talking, incoherently. Indecipherable sounds.
Beep...
The voices began to grow a little louder, some words starting to resemble real ones.
Beep...
Light creeping in, and darkness fading.
Beep...
She eased her eyes open, and let the light filter in.

A plain white ceiling stared back at her. She rolled her head to the side, trying to catch a glimpse of the room, but her head pounded at that, telling her it didn't like it. She moved it back to where it was. The beeping sound continued to echo, as she became aware of a pulling and pricking sensation on her arm. She reached down with her other hand, and felt a small bulk attached to her wrist. An IV drip. She looked upwards again to the smooth white-washed plaster, in search of answers.
It didn't offer any.

Then some approaching footsteps offered some hope, and they soon turned into a physical form, which loomed large over her. Looking down at her was neither a doctor, nor someone she recognised. Not medical staff, or someone from her organisation. This could be bad. She prepared herself as best she could, which wasn't much. Her body still didn't seem too keen on the whole moving thing. His blue eyes and unusually rounded nose stole the attention away from what was an otherwise handsome face.

Hildur didn't know what to say, but the stranger did.

'Hey, you're awake! The doctor said you would come round soon. How do you feel?'

She blinked a few times and tried to sit up, awkwardly. 'I... erm...'

Words wouldn't come.

'It's ok, take it easy.' He leant behind her and slid another pillow in so she could sit up.

'Wha... what?...' was all she could muster up before the dryness in her throat and mouth glued everything shut again.

The man handed her some water from her bedside, and continued, 'Yes, I know I know. It was all my fault. I'm so sorry! I just wasn't looking for those few seconds and fiddling about with the radio.'

'I didn't... hear—'

'Hear me coming? I did wonder.'

Hildur thought back to the distraction.

'They are just so quiet at low speed, these new Teslas. They sold it as a plus point. Clearly not always a good thing. Either way, I still should have been paying more attention. I take full blame.'

She looked at him, and blinked a few more times, trying to process all this new information.

After all the precautions taken and the possible risks that were identified, a civilian playing around with their car radio had not been one of them.

Refined to kill, and on mission number one, she had been felled by an electric car.

She let that sink in for a moment.

Her pride began to feel as bruised and as heavy as her head.

Before she could respond, the doctor walked in.

'Good to see you awake, Miss. Perfectly timed for the end of my coffee break.' The humour didn't quite match the mood of the room. 'So, how are you feeling?' Before she could reply, he continued monologuing, 'I think you're looking pretty sharp, all things considered. It was a minor knock to the head, just some mild concussion is all,' he said as he placed his icy hands on her cheeks and shone a bright light into her eyes. 'Your vital signs are all but back to normal for the last few hours, and looking far better now than when you came in,'

Her visitor opened his mouth, but it was second to the doctors again. 'So, maybe give it an hour or two, then you're free to go. And take some Lýsi for your vitamin D, that'll brighten you up! But perhaps come back again in a few days for a once over, to make sure nothing has fallen off, aye?'

He had delivered the last line with a smile, which was reciprocated from one of them, but more out of politeness than anything.

'Well, I will leave you two to it, I must go see some other patients. Some guy upstairs ran over his wife's foot, can you believe that?! And she isn't best pleased I can tell you... anyway, this coffee isn't going to drink itself. I must get to it. Madam, Sir...'

He finished with a lingering pause and slid out of the room. Silence filled the void.

'That was – ' her visitor began.

'Strange,' she finished with.

'Strange indeed, but good news though. Doctors here can be a little...' he paused, thinking how to phrase the next part, 'lackadaisical, I guess you could say,'

His smile faded and he suddenly looked awkward, averting his gaze and shifted on his feet.

'So, before the ambulance came, I was checking to see that you weren't seriously injured, making sure there wasn't any bleeding or anything, and...'

He stepped a little closer, reaching into his inside coat pocket, and pulled the items out.

'I found these.'

In his palm, lay Hildur's syringe that she had held just a few hours previously.

And in the other, her SIG Sauer pistol.

Her stomach now felt more uncomfortable than her head. A tight stitch of dread, balling up inside.

'I wanted to ask you first, I wanted to be sure, before handing this into anyone,' he said with a tone of expectancy.

Hildur had to fight to get words out. She was more awake now, memories coming to her quicker, along with excuses to get herself out of this. But she needed a little more time to think.

She also wanted to have this conversation elsewhere, away from her laying stationary in a hospital bed. She wanted to be ready to resolve this, if she failed to be convincing. She would have to find other persuasive means to convince him not to talk.

'I really need some fresh air, and some coffee,' Hildur said, now fully upright. 'Let's talk about it then.'

Her visitor thought for a moment, and replied, 'OK, sure. I'm Lars by the way,' he said holding out his hand. She shook it and smiled.

'Hildur.'

6

The Things You Found

Having had a couple of hours to restore something resembling normality in her appearance and mood, she left her room and made her way to the meeting spot. A humble place in the harbour, a coffee shop holding all of six people.
Rush hour in Reykjavik.

She arrived early and waited, looking out across the calm and motionless water, with Mt Esja holding centre stage, with all of its grandeur. There wasn't really any other option than to look at, seeing as it hogged most of the skyline for itself. So peaceful, so serene. And most of all away from here, where potential problems lay. She found herself feeling slightly envious of the towering landscape.

There also remained the need for a difficult call with her Handler. And it had the potential to be far more than awkward – awkward was the best case scenario.
But... one problem at a time.
She had a more immediate one to deal with, a problem that could not be allowed to spiral out of control, to let itself be known to anyone else, and a problem that rounded the corner,

with Lars headed straight for her. Hildur always liked it when problems brought themselves to her. They had a propensity to build if not dealt with early on.

They sat inside, tucked away in the corner, at a window facing out towards the harbour.

Hildur positioned them so that she had a good view of the entire room and the door – a habit that couldn't be suppressed even if she wanted to. She looked out again across the water.

Mt Esja continued to look down at her, smugly.

The coffees arrived, along with the questions.

'So, how are you feeling? You look a little brighter,'

'Yeah, getting there. Head is a little sore still, but I'll be ok.'

More apologies came her way, and she sent them back with insistence that it wasn't necessary. She wanted to steer the conversation to why they were really there, and after a pause from them both, she began, 'So... the things you found,'

He stiffened upright at the words, and his eyes narrowed. He put his coffee down and waited for the next part.

'I can only imagine where your mind has gone with that. Mine would have been thinking up all sorts of things too,'

He gave a slight nod but didn't speak. He still had a heavy weight in his expression.

'It's not what it seems. It's complicated to explain, and to be honest, I can't explain. It's... confidential,'

He shifted uneasily in his chair, leaning back and upright, and exhaled. Frustrated. It was going to take more than this to convince him; and she needed to. The alternative didn't bear thinking about.

She needed to offer more.

'What I can tell you, is that I work in security, as such. I cannot tell you much more than that. It's highly sensitive information, and if this were to get out, well... It wouldn't end well for me.'

Or you.

Lars looked a little more accepting of this, but still not entirely happy. Nothing she could say could get him to that point. She just had to hope that it was enough.

He sighed, and gave a reluctant, 'OK,' and then looked pensive. He thought on something for a moment, with it visually weighing him down, and then he said, 'Was anyone hurt?'

Hildur took a pause, to get the words in the right order.

'Lars – I cannot tell you who I really am, or what I do. If I did, it could harm both of us and anyone we know. I need you to forget what you know about me, and not say anything to anyone. Ever.' She leant forward, keeping direct eye contact, 'But, I will say this: I promise you that no innocent was or will be hurt on my watch.'

The words settled on him, easing in slowly, and he relaxed in his posture. He sat back, slouched in his chair. 'OK. You have my word.'

Hildur tried not to show off her relief too much, and bottled it inside.

One problem down; one to go.

With the mood lightened and a change of subject needed, Lars asked questions about her; where she grew up and where she had been. She skipped over most with vague answers, but had to give way on some, so as not to be rude. That balance between politeness and vagueness.

'I spent a lot of time in Norway and Sweden, studying,' which was true to an extent, leaving out many other details.

'Nice, what did you study?'

Her mind flashed back to an early session with her trainer, Atli. Learning how it was more efficient to stomp-kick a man's kneecap in on itself than it was to throw punches. Squared up to one another, hands raised either side of their jaws, circling, Atli demonstrated.

"Listen Hildur, I like your effort, but efficiency will get the better of effort every time."

He dodged in and immediately back out, throwing her off balance. He flew back in and knocked her to the ground.

23

"See? Work smarter, not harder," Atli always pointed out the weak spots of the body. He lived off weak spots. Hildur climbed back up and mirrored him once more, the rotating stand-off continuing. "Punches are up high, and in the eyeline of the defender. They are expected, and almost impossible to disguise," he said as he jabbed at Hildur, which she easily stepped back from.

"A quick low kick will take 'em by surprise, and they have to shift their weight to avoid it. Time it well, the weight on the leg will do most of the work for you. Behind the knee to disarm; or the front for end-game." He stepped in, sweeping the back of her knee, sending her off her feet and onto her back.

She had perfected this for herself and performed it on others, but connecting with the front, not the back. The sound stayed in her mind for some time after.

She could have sworn she heard a crack reverberate around the barely audible cafe.

Her focus came back to the room with the snap, along with her answer.

'Biology.'

He proceeded to tell her about his studies and life, and she half listened. She used the saved cognitive function to think about her next steps. How and what to explain to her Handler about this delay. What could she leave out? Some of it she had to. Would they find out? She forced herself back to the present conversation, and put the rest to the side for now. Her head still hammered away at trying to do both.

The conversation came to a natural end, and Hildur excused herself, saying she needed to rest, which was partially true. She also had things to work through. She left him in the corner of the cafe and headed out, the warm rays striking her face, springing her optic nerves and brain to life.

She walked a short way to the end of the dock, and took a moment to settle. Replayed things in her mind, checking for any errors. Evaluating her answers, and his. No alarm bells rang, and she relaxed. She stood at the end of the walkway, facing the empty vastness across the water once again. Only half an hour had passed, but it felt a lot colder.

The silence was just beginning to make itself comfortable, when it was sliced in half by a voice.

'Hildur?'

A voice she recognised, and a voice that shouldn't be here. Couldn't be here.

She turned to match it with a face, which it did. The voice was that of her Handler, no longer on the other end of the phone, but stood before her in the flesh.

The air was definitely colder now.

7

No Such Thing

With words failing her for the second time in one day, Hildur stood rooted to the spot, eyes locked on the person before her. Standing around six feet tall, in a long jet-black overcoat, and her long dark blonde hair running parallel, Maren looked her usual regal self; Hildur still a touch dishevelled.

Their appearances somewhat matched their moods and circumstances.

Hildur had failed to confirm the completion of the job, what with being unconscious. It was standard procedure, so Maren would have assumed Hildur was M.I.A for the last however many hours and flown out quickly.

But she was here now, and would soon find out all that was to be found.

What does she know already?

With Hildur still searching for words, her Handler helped her out.

'Well, he was quite the looker, wasn't he? You've done well for yourself in such a short time,'

Hildur smiled, relieved the mood had been lightened a little.

'So, I think I am up to date on what happened, the hospital staff were quite helpful with that. But I have to ask... was it done? Did you complete your task before your accident?'

Hildur pictured the fearful eyes again, realising their fate while looking into Hildur's.

'Of course. All went according to plan, apart from, you know... the car incident,'

'What happened?'

'I just looked away for a second, and apparently so did he. Just really bad luck I guess.'

Maren considered this. She knew this already, but she wanted to hear it from Hildur herself. Maren was thorough in her work, and there was no such thing as a detail too many.

'After all that training, on your first assignment, a car? Maren asked in disbelief, probing that little bit more. 'Did something else distract you?'

Does she know?

Hidlur felt a swell of heat rise to her face and tried to not avoid eye contact – but couldn't help it. Her eyes dropped at the words, just for a split second, which said plenty in itself. She brought them straight back up again, trying to hold her resolve.

'I've updated everyone on what happened, including Magnus. He was worried you know,'

Hildur found that hard to believe and fought to say nothing of it. Her father never showed worry. She pictured him with the others, receiving the news, and trying not to show his embarrassment, or making a joke of it.

Her Handler interrupted the image, 'But, what is more important than what happened then, is what happened in there?'

Maren looked past Hildur's shoulder, at the cafe where she had been with Lars, and then back to Hildur for an answer.

'Well, as I'm sure you know by now, the man who hit me accompanied me to the hospital. He naturally wanted to see that I was OK, and to apologise.'

'And,' Maren began, 'Did he have any questions? More importantly, did he find anything on you, or suspect anything?'

Maybe she doesn't know. Moment of truth...

Hildur's demeanour stayed as calm as the water at her back, as she said 'No, he didn't say or ask anything like that. I doubt he would have gone searching my pockets while I was laying there unconscious. He just wanted to make sure I was OK.'

Maren kept her gaze on Hildur, unmoving.

'He doesn't know anything, Maren,' Hildur said as she matched her Handler's gaze, and said no more. She couldn't. Talking too much in a situation like this often looked guilty. Hildur clung on to the hope and fact of how she had been Maren's favourite over the years, looking out for her when needed. She desperately needed to be her favourite again now.

'OK,' Maren conceded with a pause, 'You know I had to ask. I trust your instincts on this.'

She eased off on the physical posture, which made Hildur relax, and she let out a breath that she hadn't realised she was holding.

'The next job is now confirmed, it's good to go. We have them pinpointed. You'll have backup, but we need boots on the ground too. We want one of them alive for questioning, if possible. Be ready tonight. You will be picked up and accompanied for the next job.'

She turned and began to walk away.

Hildur desperately wanted to ask two questions and seeing as she was fairly sure she knew the answer to the former, she asked the latter.

'Who will I be going with?'

Without looking back, her Handler replied, 'Hans,' without any trace of inflection in her voice. All very matter of fact.

Fuck. Anyone but Hans.

8

Wave After Wave

With just a few hours before the job, Hildur found herself alone for what felt like the first time in days. She couldn't bear to spend them cooped up in a room, somewhere outside was needed.

She walked away from the cafe, cutting through quiet backstreets of downtown, away from the harbour, and soon came out the other side. Before long she was at the edge of the forest again, retracing her footsteps from a few hours ago. She veered off and headed in a different direction.

One of the few places she remembered of Reykjavík was its forest, which surrounded the highest peak in the downtown area. Atop the hill was a large dome-shaped building, one that she didn't remember. What was once a play area as a child was now what looked to be a large tourist attraction. A belt line of Rock Pine and Alaska Ash offered a small refuge from what was an otherwise open and exposed city.

She headed up one of the many choices of pathways, and circled around a short while, in a circuitous route, taking her to the epicentre of the woodland.

Lesser-trodden tracks lead off in several directions away from the main path, offering what seemed to be limitless paths. She chose one at random, and descended down, deeper into the heart of the forest. It twisted and turned through the trees, with the path becoming more and more unclear, until a small opening appeared. In its centre, a cluster of boulders covered in the indigenous Icelandic moss, something she remembered fondly from her childhood. It was one of the few things she did.

She sat, hands resting either side, gripping the moss, focusing on its spongy carpet-like comfort. She exhaled fully and closed her eyes. For the first time since being here, she had time to think. Stillness in the storm. True silence.

A few minutes passed.
It was time.

She let the thoughts and questions crash in, wave after wave, a messy haze of disorder. She put aside the ones of least importance – for now – and ordered the rest in terms of urgency. And then by consequence. One question then sat at the top, above all others. *Had she covered her tracks sufficiently?* And sitting in close second was: *Would they follow Lars to question him, and if they did, would he stay true to his word?*
Hildur ran through possible consequences if what had happened came to light, how Maren and those above her would react, and what her options would be then.
They multiplied and became almost impossible to keep track of.
She shut them down and put them to the side, and just focused on what she was in control of at that precise moment: her breathing.
Hildur had a few hours before needing to be in operational form – her life could depend on it. Her head still hummed with certain movements, protesting at the lack of rest. She promised it would get some later.

For now, she had to forget that she might potentially be exposed, by Lars, hospital staff, or anyone else who may have seen her. Authorities becoming aware of TESS' presence would complicate things to an unbelievable degree. And with it, raise more questions: *would TESS back her, or leave her to escape herself?*

They have distanced themselves as much as possible in the past from being discovered. At any hint of being implicated, they have cut ties with assets.

She didn't want to think of that possibility any further and got up.

She left her newfound sanctuary of solitude and headed up the path, soon coming to the top. Partly for the views, but it also offered the quickest way back to her place.

She passed dog walkers on the way, a few runners, and couples out for a walk. All getting on with their innocent lives. Some of them were probably dealing with problems of their own too. She wondered if any of them would be interested in switching. *Probably not.*

A runner flew past her, a woman in her thirties. She couldn't help but catch the scent of her perfume. Jasmine-based, one of her favourites. A little unusual to run with perfume on, perhaps a remnant from its original application. Or maybe people just like to look and smell good all the time. She had seen such things in gyms before, people posing more than working out. Of this, she had no experience herself. All exercises had been undertaken with full commitment, often covered in blood and bruises, sometimes broken bones. Those were the bad days. Maybe one day she would put something nice on, and go to a gym, like normal people did.

Almost at the top of the hill, she passed more people. The runners and dog-walkers thinned out, leaving couples who were out for a stroll. And then a singleton, a man walking by himself, wearing a puffy jacket, workman's trousers, and

33

sturdy boots. He was kitted out well for hiking, that was for sure. More ready for a mountain peak than a low-incline path.

Hildur usually found that if people were out by themselves, they tended to be on their phone, or have headphones in. He had neither. At second glance, Hildur noticed the attire was not local, which wouldn't have been worth noting, if it weren't for the fact that he looked nothing like a tourist. And he was unusually focused and attentive.

Time to test.

As they passed one another, she glanced his way, wearing half a smile whilst tucking hair behind her hair – that little bit extra to catch the eye. The man didn't as much as flinch. He just looked straight ahead, and went on past.

She should have expected as much.

The people they were watching were watching them too.

9

Headed For The Hills

Having slipped away from the forest and out of the watch of whoever it was, Hildur made a call and relayed the information to Maren, and returned to her place.

She circled the building where she was staying three times, in both directions, randomly turning back every now and then to surprise anyone who tried to follow her. It gave her sufficient time to scan house and car windows for potential threats.

After finding none, she finally entered, and had de-clothed by the time she reached the bedroom.

She wasn't sure which she had needed the most, the nap or the shower. Whichever one it was, she soaked in every last second from both. They had been in short supply lately, and she wasn't going to waste a second of either.

Apart from a momentary loss of balance in the shower, Hildur's concussion had all but gone. The embarrassment, however, lingered on in force. She had taken far worse knocks and recovered far quicker. Not to mention the manner in which it happened. After fitting into some sports gear, she set about her daily workout routine, doing an additional twenty percent on each set. The dizziness tried to make itself present again, but she answered it by pushing through with more repetitions.

Workout finished, and a second shower, she wandered through the empty rooms of the apartment. The silent void enticed her to replay it over again, to pick at the details. She suppressed it, putting it to a corner of her mind. She had to have full focus for what was coming. She hit shuffle on a random Spotify playlist and threw the phone onto the bed, which sprung back up, along with some new-age hit about some boy missing a girl, and so on. Everyone knew the rest.

After changing, Hildur waited outside for all of two minutes before her ride arrived.
The electric motor came to a stop less than a metre from her, and Hildur froze for an instant at the sight, stuck to the spot by the flashback. The memory and image before her were almost a carbon-copy.
A dark blue Tesla.
Hans climbed out, with his usual smug smile and unnecessary sunglasses. She wasn't sure which one was more annoying.

'Hey Hilly,' he said, as the smile got wider, along with a wink. Now she knew which one it was.
He was annoyingly handsome. She wasn't annoyed at him for being handsome, but at the fact that he was fully aware of it.
'What's with the stupid car?' Hildur replied.
'This? Come on, you're just jealous,' Hans said as he shut the door, circling around it, whilst keeping his eyes on it at all times in a lustful fashion.
Hildur wondered if they needed a minute together, alone.
'Heard things didn't go so smoothly for you, and the cavalry had to be called for backup,' Hans said as he delicately ran a finger along the side of the bodywork, his gaze still captivated.
Hildur definitely didn't want to be around if this went any further.

'The backup isn't to *help* me; you and others are needed here anyway. And what happened to me was a freak accident. Just bad luck. And I don't need anyone's help because of it.'
Especially yours.
'OK, OK! Hans blurted out as he held his hands up, patting the air in a defensive manner, 'Nice to see you too. Come on, let's get in. We have some miles to do.'
As tempting as it was to get in the back, she resisted and got in the passenger seat. She'd had enough confrontation for now.

They pulled out of the quiet roads, barely adding any sound to the night with the electric motor.
'Can you believe they have these in Iceland?! Newest and top of the range, on this little island. Who'da thought?! Didn't know they were so fancy here,' he said as he fiddled with some gadgets on the dashboard, which seemed to do nothing, and added 'Couldn't resist, had to get me one,'
Of course you did.

Hans always had the propensity to be the centre of attention, with that flare and flash. Hildur doubted much of that had changed in the six months since she last saw him. They had a somewhat tumultuous rivalry, the two of them excelling in training exercises ahead of most others, competing for best times and distances covered. The last time out they had been the only two to reach the top of Lofoten mountain in Norway, ego pushing one of them on, and determination the other.
They each had their fair share of wins, but showed it in different ways.
Hildur preferred to be humble in victory.
Hans shouted from the rooftops.

'Spoken to your father?' Hans asked.
'No, why would I?'
'Well, about what happened yesterday. News probably reached him by now. Maybe he—'
'*He* doesn't give a shit, and it doesn't concern him. So drop it.'

Hans looked away from her and eased off, 'Okay! Okay. Won't mention it again.'

They left the sprawling roads of the capital and edged away from the hue of the city and headed for the hills and the darkness.

10

Stickler For Standards

Maren had her latte sent back for the second time, on account of it not being hot enough.

The first time was a calamity, but the second time was a sham.

Cold milk in a barely hot drink was unacceptable to her, and an easy task to remember. A stickler for standards, she made those around her rise to meet her own.

After thanking the barista, she glided through a small crowd that waited behind, which parted quickly. While imposing in size, it was her gait and demeanour that demanded attention from people the most.

She beckoned Jakob to follow her with a motion of the finger, and he cut off his call and did as told.

'Ma'am, we've got eyes on them, Lucas and Sven are monitoring. He's with his family,'

Jakob spluttered as he jogged to keep up with Maren's lengthy stride.

'Good, we keep watch. We will talk with him when there is a good opportunity.'

'Do you trust what Hildur said, Ma'am?'

Maren slowed her pace, and now looked at him as she spoke, 'If there is anyone I trust the most out of all of you, it's *her*,' she said with a weight of emphasis on the final word.

Before he could reply, Maren's phone rang, and from her facial expression, Jakob knew who it was, and stayed silent.

'Wait in the car, Jakob.'

For the second time, he did as he was told, and got in.

Maren looked at the caller ID. She let the phone ring for longer than she usually would, especially given who the caller was. She didn't like to keep him waiting.

No one did.

Maren rarely faltered or let emotions attach themselves to her, and there weren't many who had the capacity to inflict unease onto her – he was about the only one. After more than ten years of working with him, she still feared his unpredictability. The spearhead of TESS, he ran the rule over all those who worked for the organisation with unwavering ruthlessness.

Having steadied herself, Maren answered the call.

'Sir,' Maren began, 'we have a confirmed kill from Hildur, and the next phase is under way. We have sights on all of their crew, and our people are in position to finish this.'

Maren waited for a response, as most people did with him; they did the talking, he did the judging.

Her nerves made her restless, and she walked at a slow pace towards the dock.

'Good,' the man finally replied.

The subsequent silence was a cue for Maren to give more information.

'We have been monitoring their HQ for the last 24 hours, and we have confirmation. There's lots of activity inside, high heat-signatures, multiple frequencies. There must be a shit load of electricals inside, it has to be it. We will try to salvage what we can after we take the place, but any data they have on us, they could have backups elsewhere. We—'

'Yes, good,' the man interjected. Maren stayed quiet and waited for him to continue.

'A situation has come to attention, Maren, and it needs to be dealt with. Promptly.'

Maren stopped walking and swallowed hard.

'Yes, Sir, I am aware. I have a solution for this, I – '

'No,' the man said, cutting her off for a second and final time.

'I will *tell* you the solution.'

11

Endless Roads

The Icelandic landscape began to roll on and on, illuminated by the gentle midnight glow. The horizon had merged into a mixed gradient of colours, ranging from dark orange to dark blue. They had swapped buildings for mountains, and traffic lights for what seemed like endless roads.

After an hour of driving, they were well and truly out of the city's reach. It never took long in Iceland to find isolation. A solitary car would pass at ten minute intervals, and they were becoming less frequent. Hans' attempt at constant conversation had died down, but still came up once in a while. Hildur kept the responses to a minimum where possible. Sometimes he was more persistent than others, and she had to give a little out of politeness, but more out of boredom.
Hans started again.

'Seriously, how are you feeling? You don't quite look your normal self. There's no shame in admitting if you're still feeling the effects from it.'
Hildur straightened up at the suggestion, suddenly conscious of her slouched physical posture.

'Hans,' Hildur began with, and paused to phrase it carefully. 'I've had much worse. If it was bothering me, I would say. The hospital gave me the all-clear anyway.'

Hans eased his tone, and replied 'I know you're fine physically; I mean... Is there anything else? You seem unusually distracted, even for someone who just took a whack to the head,'

It pulled at her again, willing her to relive it.

Maybe she could tell him something. A part of it at least. He would find out sooner or later anyway.

Hildur sighed, and said 'I wasn't alone, after I was hit and at the hospital,'

Hans glanced her way.

'The guy who hit me with the car, he came with me to the hospital, and... he found my gun on me, and the syringe. They must have fallen from my jacket when I hit the floor,' the words began to pain her to get them out. Saying it out loud like this felt like another blow with every word, heavy, and excruciating.

'I spoke with him after, explained that I was security, of sorts. He knows the consequences if he were to talk about it, and he gave his word that he wouldn't.'

'And, does Maren know?'

'She knows I spoke with him for a while, but not that he found a gun on me.'

Hans took his eyes off the road again, this time his stare more severe, 'So, you lied to her?'

'I had no ID on me, so the hospital can't trace me. And as long as Lars doesn't talk, then none of this can come back to TESS,'

'Lars?' Hans said as he raised his eyebrows at her, questioning the use of the first name.

Hildur ignored it.

'So, he found you with a gun, close to where someone was killed, in a nation where there is a murder about once per decade?' Hans asked rhetorically, the question jabbing at Hildur harder still.

'Then let's hope you did a good job clearing up your mess,' Hans said, looking at her again.

Hildur looked away and out of the window.

'Either that or hope that he's as thick as pig shit and can't put two and two together,' Hans said, snickering at his own joke, before asking 'Do you trust him to keep quiet?'

'Yes,'

She paused.

'Then what's the problem?' Hans asked.

'I don't trust that Maren trusts it. I think she could... *talk* with him. And if she knows what he found, she might... He has a family, Hans, she can't find out,'

Hans considered it, and said 'Well, if she does, let's hope it's just a *talk*.'

They turned off the paved road, and headed up a gravel one. Before long, they were deep into the ancient lava field, which was covered in moss. To their left, a volcano stood in solitude, with more up ahead. None of them were exceptional in size, but would have caused considerable damage in their heyday, the sprawling leftover lava fields being the testament.

Hans pulled over and put the car in park, out of sight of the landscape ahead. He opened his door, and said, 'We go on foot from here.'

They began their hike through the field, the tangerine-tinged horizon lighting the way. The terrain remained mainly flat, with the occasional drop where the gaps and crevices lay in the lava. Some were big enough to stumble down, others large enough to fit a car down, never to be found.

Hildur stepped on the rock hard substance where possible, while Hans walked directly over the spongy moss, and delighted in the fact.

'This stuff is so soft! Wouldn't mind hikin' on this all the time.'

Hildur tensed at the sight.

'You shouldn't walk on that,'

45

'Oh yeah, and why's that?'

Hildur thought back to some of the Icelandic folklore, about the hidden people, Elves, and lives being claimed by them and the land, never to be seen again.

'Because you could end up in it.'

Hans hesitated a beat, before carrying on.

'Pfft! Whatever.'

'I'm serious Hans,' she said at the risk of sounding like her Mother, 'be careful... or the land will take you.'

They ascended a small hill, and slowed as they neared the top. In the distance, vast mountains stood side by side, blotting out the sun. And between that and them, still a vast expanse. And a short way into that expanse, a shape was just about visible. A building with no lights on, but compromised by the night sky's incandescence. An old and decrepit building that would have appeared to most to be empty, but not to Hans and Hildur. They knew exactly what lay inside the old rotten bricks before them.

Some of the most dangerous people on the planet.

They continued on, down towards the building, eyes flicking between the path and the target. No sign of lights, and no movement. If they hadn't been told, they would have been sure the place was empty.

As they approached, she expected Hans to try and give some orders, to say that he would take point, or to tell her which entrance to use – his usual bossy self. But he didn't. He remained as silent as the night around them.

They both paused a few beats, focusing fully on their surroundings – for any noises or movement. There were none.

They closed the last remaining distance between them and the house. They positioned themselves at the front door, as it was just as good as any at this point. The element of surprise was on their side.

Guns drawn, Hans leant across and tried the handle, which turned at first ask, pushed it open, and Hildur burst inside.

12

Into The Night

With her eyes aiming down the iron-sights, her arms and gaze swept across the room from left to right, and back to the centre again.

The scan revealed a space some forty feet deep to the back wall, and twenty feet across. Dimly lit, and would have been cold if it weren't for the stacks of electrical equipment warming the place.

Some of the towers were six feet high, humming and flashing away. Screens filling in all the spaces between, all linked up to make one large infrastructure. Top of the range Wi-Fi routers were flanked by cloud storage servers, and enough hard drives to store information on all the citizens of Europe three times over.

All the computing power and equipment necessary to do a lot of damage, if used by the right people. People such as Fenrir. While TESS took the fight to their opponents by turning up at their doorsteps, Fenrir slipped in through the back door of their electrical equipment, most of the time unnoticed. Fenrir also carried with them financial might, partially gained through

Bitcoin mining. And with a setup such as this, they had an ever-growing bankroll to challenge TESS with.

The setup had everything – everything except for one thing.

The people.

Hans had filtered in behind, carrying out an almost identical sweep, give or take a few stylistic and physical nuances. The room was silent.

The building... was silent.

Hans and Hildur looked at one another but didn't say anything. As annoying as Hans was, he was a good operator. He stepped past Hildur and took point, gun sight aimed high and forward the whole time. Hildur kept hers aimed at the door they had entered through.

Hans signalled to move forward, and they did in a pair, both constantly sweeping in a 180 degree motion to maintain full protective coverage as a unit. They'd practiced it many times - she never thought she'd be having to do it with him, here, for real.

They moved up the stairs, to find one big attic, with several mattresses scattered across the floor. Four in total, but some bedding was half-packed away, and with a sofa, too, there was potential for up to six.

Full scan complete, and with the building empty, Hans spoke.

'They knew we were coming.'

'No, not possible,' Hildur replied.

'Well, there's no other explanation for it, they wouldn't just up and leave all this shit, would they? All of this is their weapon.'

'They—' Hildur began, before she cut off her own trail of thought.

'They what?' Hans asked.

Hildur's eyes glared wide as it hit her. It played back in her mind again, this time not able to keep it out. The realisation of that small possibility that she had put to one side, might have happened. And if it had… Hildur didn't want to think about what it could bring.

'Hildur?' Hans asked as he peered out of the window, and after getting no reply, continued, 'they can't have gone far, no sign of fresh tyre marks outside. They're on foot, and they have nowhere to go out there, except to hide in that weird grass.'

Moss.

Hildur was now at the window looking out, still running it through her mind. The possibility. It was small, but it was there; and it would explain what was happening now.

'Be sharp Hills,' Hans said, 'they could be watching us,'

Hildur listened intently before Hans went to speak, and for the first time, she cut him off.

'Quiet,' she ordered.

They listened.

It was faint, and not particularly recognizable, but it was there. A humming, whirring sound, growing clearer and louder. Not so much of a humming anymore, it was more of a droning.

A sudden sharp whistling noise came next, as Hildur yelled to get out, and jumped towards the window, the shockwave from behind sending her through with ease.

Hildur, along with a million fragments of glass flew outward into the night, and to the ground below.

The building – what was left of it – was in ruins.

13

Killing Machine

Hildur opened her eyes to see flames flicking and dancing towards the sky, providing some competition for the night-time sun.

The flames were winning by some way.

She heaved debris from herself and rolled onto her back. Above the fierce crackling sounds of the fire, she could just about make out the sound from before, in the background.

And then she saw it.

It hovered overhead, still aiming at the building, circling around, surveying.

A drone.

Time to RAM: regain control, assess the situation, and move.

She lay still, moving nothing but her eyes, keeping track of the killing machine.

She rested everything else, paying attention to all parts of her body, assessing the damage. Nothing felt broken, but it was almost impossible to tell, as it could be masked with adrenaline and shock. She moved each part, slowly, gradually increasing each movement.

She was ready to move. She had to. The drone still hummed up above, still searching for heat signatures. It would be a tough task given the heat coming from the burning structure. She waited until it went behind the building, until she was concealed, and sprang up and ran.

Hildur sprinted for a small hillside overlooking the scene. A short distance to cover, perhaps a ten second sprint. After a few strides – which were more like uneven lunges – it became apparent to her it was going to be more. Her left ankle was damaged, as were her ribs.

She covered the distance in fifteen, then spun and lay flat on the ground, and fixed her eyes straight on the drone. It had just arrived at where she had been lying, and hadn't tracked her run. She was safe.
For now.
The next task lay in wait: find the drone operator.

The drone was a quadcopter model, although larger than the usual type due to it carrying a small missile launcher. It wouldn't have been easy to bring into the country in sections, but do-able. With it being the model that it was, it had limited capabilities. It had the capacity to fire just one rocket, which it had done already. Threat level lowered. There was a possibility that it would have a small gun attachment, but she couldn't be sure. What it definitely could do was to give away not only her position, but the fact that she was alive.

Hildur continued to scan the area, a few seconds at a time, and then back on the UAV. With it still remaining fixed on the building, her focus went on to scan a new area. She sat still and watched. She had expected something to happen by now, but nothing. And just as she started to doubt her theory, she saw it. Not where she was looking, but in her peripheral vision.
Movement.

Several figures were moving in the distance, just about visible, appearing almost static relative to Hildur's position. They were trying to keep low, but their desire and instinct for speed was taking over, which compromised them.

They had been hiding in the hills, watching things unfold. Hildur and Hans approach, storm in, and then their building and work go up in flames. Amongst all of that burning equipment would probably be a smouldering long-distance motion sensor, which was their heads up and chance for escape.

Having found them, step one was complete, and, as she was wondering if step two would present itself, it did almost instantly. Around half a kilometre to the right of the runners, the drone operator shifted in their position. Not out of necessity, but out of excitement. Poor patience.

With her eyes flicking between the two targets, she chose, and headed for the hill.

14

Fight Against The Heat

With her injuries hindering her speed, Hildur arced her run to loop around the back, instead of the more direct run that she would have otherwise taken. It gave her a little more time to take stock of the damage. The pain in the rib-cage remained steady, but the ankle worsened with each step. Probably a mild strain, which her adrenalin would get her through. The dizziness, however, had made a comeback.

Every few strides she corrected her path, and focused on stabilising herself.

She couldn't afford too many more falls.

With half the distance covered, Hildur noticed the UAV change direction, and make its way across the plain towards the runners. Had the operator not been so focused on his screen and trusted his own eyes more, he would have seen Hildur barrelling towards him. But he didn't.

She slowed on the approach, and crouched down, easing each foot down into each step. The soft ground below of chewed up rock and lava helped conceal the sound, keeping her presence undetected right until the last second. Opting against a fatal blow, Hildur made a deliberate sound, pressing down hard on the ground, causing the man in front to turn his head.

Halfway through the turn, she struck him with an open-palm chop to the Vagus nerve on the side of the neck, tricking the brain momentarily into thinking the blood pressure was too high, and the brain then trying to balance it out – by shutting it down. He flopped to the ground in an instant, and remained motionless.

Hildur stood looking over her work, the drone operating screen, and the runners below. She turned her attention to the screen, and saw that the drone remained in the air, hovering as an almost casual fixture in the night sky.

With a few flicks of the toggles, she got to grips with the directions, and aimed it to where she wanted it to go. Not towards the runners, but back towards the engulfed structure.

It still outshone the luminous night sky, raging away against the mountainous backdrop. The drone images showed that some walls inside had fallen away, collapsing in the fight against the heat. She moved the focus to the outside, and scanned the ground in the surrounding areas. There was mostly debris covering it all, some on fire, some not. She aimed at where she had been laying, and zoomed in more. A small clearance remained where she had landed. Glass, wood, and some shattered concrete was scattered all around.

She moved it farther on, searching the next pile of rubble. A few metres from where she had landed lay a larger mound, and from it protruded an arm, and a lower part of a leg.
A leg which began to move.

15

Past The Flames

After locating the hackers' car in an out-building, Hildur hot-wired it and bundled Hans into the back.

He was bordering on conscious, which was enough to assist with the manoeuvring so that he wasn't a complete dead-weight. She checked him over – as much as she could – for any signs of serious damage. His heart rate was within normal range, so no serious blood loss. There could be some broken bones, but that would become apparent when he regained full consciousness. For now, it looked as though he would make it through the night.

Hildur surveyed the wreckage once more, and stared into the destruction. This wouldn't be it; more would come.

She looked past the flames, searching for the runners, but they were lost to the night.

They had one hell of a journey ahead of themselves too, with nothing but long barren stretches before them. Fenrir's weapon – their computing power – was gone.

They were no threat now.

She got in the car and drove a short distance from all that had happened, putting distance between them and the faint flicker that emanated from the wreckage, until it was a low glow in the rear view mirror. She found a secluded spot and pulled up, out of sight from anyone passing on the main road, but where she could also still see the burning building.

More than half an hour passed, and no one came or went. The drone operator had been alone, with no backup. But there could be some on the way. Whoever wanted Hans and Hildur dead wouldn't stop at that, they would want to make sure the job was finished.

Hildur stopped thinking and planning, and took a deep breath, unwinding from the whirlwind that had just happened. She put her hands to her head, palms over the eyes, and then rubbed her temples, hoping that somehow it would help a little, but all it did worsen the throbbing, and sprinkled glass from her hair onto her lap.
She lowered them to her side, and forfeited an exhale.

While many urges and intuitions snapped at her very being, only one of them was successful – sleep – and she let it take her for the first time in almost 24 hours.

16

Incoming Call

Just as it seemed as though she had closed her eyes, they were opening again. She had slept more than she felt she had, as it was considerably brighter. She blinked a few times until the adjustment settled on her retinas. Although the light was vigorous, it wasn't what had woken her. It was the drone operator's phone.

It rang several times before she was conscious enough to be holding the phone up, and looking at the incoming call – random number. It rang out and returned to a home screen. Whoever was at the end of the call was at fault for the pain in her ribs, the shattered glass in her hair, a swollen ankle, and for Hans being unconscious next to her. She wasn't quite ready for that call.
Not just yet.

She pulled out her own phone to call Maren. They needed backup, someone else had been in on it, tracking them. Maybe they had missed some warning signs, maybe they hadn't been paying full attention. What had they missed? Whatever it was, they hadn't seen it, and they paid the price. They were alone, in the middle of nowhere, and injured. They had been sloppy, and they needed help.

As Hildur went to dial, a thousand splintered and refracted colours shone back at her, her phone resembling a kaleidoscope more than a smartphone. It must have helped break her fall, or was a cause of some of the bruising to her side. Whichever one, it was useless. She dropped it to the floor, and searched Hans for his: nothing. He had lost it altogether. Hildur let out a scream, which surprised even herself. She refocused and started the engine, and set off. They had to get on the move.

Glancing back to where they had been, the flames had died down to not much more than a flicker. There was some movement around the debris, vehicles circling. It was likely the emergency services had been notified by a passer-by since it happened, and they would be searching the area.

It was also likely that someone would be searching for her and Hans too, to confirm they had been removed. And '*they*', could be anyone, and anywhere. They weren't safe from anyone until they figured it out. The one thing their attackers did know is Hans and Hildur's last known location, which left them vulnerable, wounded targets, out in the open. But at least they were targets on the move now. Hildur had to get them away to a new location. Anywhere but here.

The car rolled down the gravel path, heading for the main road. Up ahead lay a split in the road, along with it an important choice to make. To the south, Reykjavik, where TESS and Maren were, and probably also whoever just blew them sky-high, or, to the West, Ólafsvík, towards a quiet peninsula where they could hide out and recuperate, and get some much-needed rest. Seeing as they couldn't contact Maren, the latter seemed the safer option of the two. Another attack was more likely on trying to return to the capital.

As they neared the junction, the phone rang again. Hildur slowed the vehicle, stared at the screen for a few seconds, before clicking answer, and waited for their saboteur to speak.

17

Help

A heavy silence surrounded the call and the car. Neither of the callers dared to break first, to give away the leverage.

Hildur grew into the silence, owning it. She was an introvert; she could do this all day. Some people couldn't bear silence, they found it awkward and had to talk through it. Not Hildur, she relished it. Just as she was getting ready to settle in for the long haul, the caller spoke first, solving two things in one sentence: losing their leverage, and eliminating the need to call her Handler.

'I hope you went easy on him, Hilly,' the words seemed to linger on for longer than they were spoken. Hildur seethed behind the earpiece, but didn't let it show.
'You know I've always hated that nickname.'
Maren ignored her response. 'So, I take it he is no longer with us. He was only surveillance, you could have spared him,' she paused, 'and Hans?'
Hildur glanced back at the damaged carcass of the man, who shifted slightly, with a small grumble.
'Dead.'

Maren let out a solemn sigh and then went quiet.

'Why him too?' Hildur asked.

'Collateral damage, I guess. But mainly because we decided he would probably side with you, given your history,'

'Our history?'

'Yes,' Maren said, 'you two always seemed... close. Combative, but close. It was always clear that he had a soft spot for you. Don't tell me you never noticed?'

Hildur felt herself starting to shake, and her vision narrowed so much that everything around became a blind spot. She had so many questions she wanted to ask, to scream. Somehow, she held them in, and Maren spoke again.

'I'm guessing you've figured it out about now?'

Hildur had, but she still didn't want to believe it. It was the smallest of things, and yet, it had come to this.

'I have, but... why like this?' Hildur asked, sure of the answer, but she wanted to hear it anyway.

'You lied to us, Hildur. Did you really think we wouldn't find out?'

Hildur couldn't stop the images replaying this time, no matter how hard she tried: ...*the needle. Primed and ready. With no reaction from the target, she moved in for the strike.*

The target turned around, and her wide eyes met with Hildur's, and froze. Hildur froze too, finding herself unable to move.

Needle up high, ready, waiting... but...

'It was only a matter of time, Hildur. You must have known that?' Maren said, snapping Hildur out of the memory. 'You knew he would act on this.'

'But you don't know, not everything. Did you even stop to think why? To ask why?'

'We didn't have to. We know you lied to us; how could we believe anything you say after that?'

Hildur couldn't argue with that. No talking could get her out of it now.

She felt empty, and defeated. She had messed up, lied to protect, and was now being held accountable, the way it should be. Hildur always faced up to her actions. Responsibility gave meaning to life, she never understood why people shied away from it.

Even if it meant it brought something to an end.

Even her end.

TESS had gone to the extreme to remove her and Hans, and they would do so again.

She had to face it – as the car rolled towards the end of the road, it was also the end of hers.

It was all over.

She sat staring ahead, just about glimpsing the ocean in the far distance. The car was down to a slow idling speed now, only just moving, her feet resting and her hand now off the wheel, slumped at her side.

Her Handler broke the silence first again.

'Look, Hildur…' her tone now changed drastically, but Hildur couldn't pinpoint to what, 'maybe he doesn't need to know about this call. Maybe, it can be just between you and me. You can disappear, and start fresh somewhere. No one will come looking for you.'

A favour, in a strange sort of way.

Even though she had made the order for Hildur's life, she still had respect for her. They were similar in some ways: ruthless when they needed to be, but still saw opportunities for kindness and knew when to take them, even at their own risk.

Hildur thought on it. She looked to the West, to the end of the jagged mountains, the volcano's glacier glistening in the morning light. She imagined being at the top, breathing fresh air, and feeling free, taking her time to heal, before heading farther North, maybe to the West Fjords, or even the highlands. The temptation bit at her. Hard. She bit her tongue instead. There was no going back from this decision.

But before she made it, one question remained.

'And,' Hildur said, 'what of Lars, and his family?'

'That isn't your concern now.'

'Answer the question Maren,' Hildur ordered sternly.

'You know his decision. He decided on dealing with this problem by removing all of the problems, and I can't stop that.'

The car now rolled to a complete stop, resting at the junction for the West and South. Hildur looked South, towards the Capital, and pictured him, unknowingly surrounded by danger. Her hit-and-not-runner, husband and father. *A father playing with his kids in the garden, BBQ ablaze, daylight filling the place. His wife laughing and cheering the kids on. They catch him and he falls, and they climb on him, claiming the victory. A peaceful home, a free family, happy and independent.*

Innocent.

He looks up at her from under the cluster of kids, and the joy is lost for a moment. There is sorrow in his face, as if he knows. He doesn't say it out loud, he doesn't have to, because his face does all the talking. A face that is clearer now than when it was closeup from the hospital bed. A face that spoke one simple word.

Help.

'Hildur?'

The only response she got was a dead dial tone, as Hildur smashed her foot down on the accelerator, turned the wheel, and spun up dust and dirt over the sign for Ólafsvík.

18

A Rare Sign

Maren tapped on the steering wheel, while alternating from looking at her phone to through the windshield. A rare sign of anxiousness from her. Jakob couldn't ever remember seeing her like this. He had returned to the car as the call finished, and was unsure of the situation. He trod lightly.

'Ma'am?'
Maren ignored him at first, finishing a thought. Whatever it was, it was a complex one. She came out of it, and said, 'We may have a problem,'
Jakob went to speak, but was interrupted by Maren's phone.
He knew who it would be, and knew to stay quiet.
Maren exhaled, answered, and spoke first, as she knew she had to.

'The hit is confirmed, Sir. The building is in tatters, and everything inside is destroyed. All of their equipment and data, gone,'

She paused a little to give him an opening to ask, but his silence did all the questioning. She continued, 'One unplanned casualty: the drone operator. Not clear how, perhaps somehow caught up in the blaze. Not confirmed, but no answer from his phone and no movement on his GPS for several hours, it's probable he's no longer with us,'

The man on the other end finally spoke.

'That's not important right now. As long as both friendlies are confirmed?'

She felt hesitation coming. Maybe she didn't need to tell him, not just yet. Maybe she could still solve this herself. It wouldn't end well for her or Hildur if she told him how things stood at that precise moment, that the hit was unsuccessful, she was still alive, and she had no idea what Hildur was going to do next. She needed time to talk some sense into Hildur, and find out whatever it was she was planning.

'Not confirmed, but we have the data back that the drone fired, and the building was demolished,' Maren said. 'He wouldn't have fired if they weren't inside. Bodies are being pulled from the wreckage as we speak, we will get confirmation soon,'

More silence came from the other end. After a few moments, he continued, 'Call me when this is all wrapped up and confirmed. Round up what's left of the team in Reykjavik, and meet the others at the airport. We need you back in Oslo, we need to prepare for a response from Fenrir,'

'Sir, I—'

'Clean this up, Maren.'

Before she could reply, the line went dead, leaving her open-mouthed, and a pointless puff of air made its way out of her lungs, never quite forming the intended words.

A calmness took over the car, a calmness that Jakob soon ruined.

'There's no way they survived that, not a chance,' he said assuredly.

Maren finally lowered the phone, still gazing outward, her mind elsewhere.

Jakob continued, 'So we wait until they confirm it's Hildur's body, then we high-tail it out of here and back to Oslo?' he said supposedly. 'Nice and easy,'

'Yeah…' Maren began. 'About that…'

19

By Our Own

Hans stirred and shifted some more, along with some grumbles, but words were yet to come. It could be a long way back to consciousness, it took different people different times. He was getting closer.

Until that time, Hildur was alone with her thoughts and the road. The long empty straights gave her plenty of time to think. Back to the start of the mission, or even before, trying to search for warning signs amongst the memories. But none came. Maybe all of this had been inevitable up to this point. Whichever it was, they were here now; on the run from their own, and injured.

She put those thoughts behind, and focused ahead, to the road and next steps.
She mentally mapped the first few rungs of a plan, although wasn't sure what would be at the top – she would figure that out and the rest along the climb.
Before she got too deep into those particular thoughts, Hans stirred some more, along with some attempted words.

'Whaaa…errr…' Hans muttered as he lifted his head, and promptly flopped it back down again. He readjusted himself on the backseat, positioning so that he could sit upright, which he did slowly and with a wobble.

'What…' was all he managed to get out this time. Hildur did the rest of the talking.

'Take it easy, Hans. We're safe for now,'

He was sitting upright in the back now, his face fully visible in the rear-view mirror. He had cuts on his cheek, one of them fairly deep, and his hair was, for the first time, dishevelled.

A part of her was pleased to see the sight.

He ruffled his hands through his hair, and managed his first full sentence. 'What the fuck happened?'

'We were attacked by our own,'

Hans just looked at her in the reflection, Hildur still with eyes on the road.

'No,' he said defiantly. 'No, no fucking way. Why? Wh…Why would they?'

Hildur looked at him now in the mirror, their eyes meeting.

'I messed up Hans, more than you know,'

His glare intensified, as he said, 'What did you do Hildur?'

She withdrew her eyes, placing them back on the road.

Hans climbed through the gap, fumbling his way between the seats and landed as best he could in the passenger side, correcting himself soon after. He turned to look at her. 'Hildur?' He sat square-on to her, held his gaze, and waited for an answer.

Hans went to repeat himself, but Hildur felt pity and saved him the struggle. She filled him in on the few hours he had been out, the aftermath of the strike and taking out the drone operator, the call with Maren, and what had happened in the last two days in more detail.

Hans took a few moments to make sense of it all, and finally replied, 'And what now, next move?'

'We go to them. If we run, we will only be hunted. We should force this now, while they least expect it,'

'Let's contact Atli, maybe he can – '

'Do what?' Hildur said as she cut him off. 'He's a world away, he can't help us now. We can help ourselves by remembering the training he gave us,'

Hans agreed with that one.

'They might not find us,' Hans added, whilst scanning the open expanse, 'there are plenty of places to hide out here,'

'They found people who were some of the best at not being found, you really think we can do better?'

Hans considered it, his silence showing his agreeance. Hildur took her eyes from him and put them back on the road ahead, and said, 'We finish this. Now.'

20

Bumper To Bumper

The noise from the back of the car drowned out the radio, which was par for the course with two young children. The argument of who had the highest score on Angry Birds was of the utmost importance at their age. Lars considered increasing the volume, but the kids would only match it; sometimes a small victory could be gained by knowing when to accept an early defeat.

They crept forward by the inch through the downtown traffic, sometimes having the fortune of gaining two. Small victories.

It seemed that on a sunny Saturday afternoon, all denizens had the same bright idea in Reykjavik – beach. And seeing as there was only one in the area, it brought the roads to a stand-still. As always, everyone accepted this fate, and politely edged through the queues, always within inches of the next car – bumper to bumper.

Just in case they lost their precious lead.

Having eventually parked in a space that would require advanced-trigonometry to exit from later, Lars and his wife Thorrun teamed up as a tag-team duo to get the children out of the car with as little resistance as possible, which meant allowing them to remain fixated on the devices they held mere inches from the eyes; like bumper to bumper.

As they spilled out across the car park, the kids unknowingly dropped belongings behind them in a breadcrumb-trail, while Lars and Thorrun picked them up in a parental-relay fashion. They thought of it as practice for the school's family sports day – or at least they tried to.

Having successfully cleared the car park, the foursome took their place amongst the masses, and sat on the imported Moroccan golden-grains; a welcome variant from the common volcanic black-grit. As they settled, another car rolled into a spot a few spaces away from where the family had parked, and switched off the engine. A car that had followed them all through downtown, and had watched their house all morning. The two men inside sat and watched the family unpack and make themselves comfortable.

The driver reached for his phone, and made the call.

21

Fickle Nature

Reykjavik glinted in the near distance, its glass and metallic structures playing pinball with the light. Wall to wall sunshine like this in Iceland was rare, and had to be taken advantage of – and so it was.

The roads were packed, mainly coming out of the city. Nobody really went *to* the city for the weekend, they either stayed or got out.

They entered the outskirts of the city and advanced along Miklabraut, the main arterial pathway running into the heart of the city, undeterred apart from the occasional and inevitable red light.

The return journey had been decidedly quieter than the outgoing one, with Hans barely saying a word on the way back to the capital. Hildur wondered if it was because of the blows he had suffered, or if it was because of what she had told him, but she didn't ask, and let it be.

She knew him well enough to know which one it would be.

They rolled through the downtown streets, with the monolithic church towering over them as they rounded it. There was something about an illuminated church that always drew Hildur's gaze.

It was a brief moment of luxury she allowed herself, before returning to the present. The main stretch of road before them led down into the main tourist area, past bars, restaurants, and souvenir shops. A place where locals and tourists mingled as one, although today the former heavily outweighed the latter. Out in their droves, groups drinking craft ales, as well as the sun. Music made its way out of one establishment, particularly pronounced, which trickled through the crack of the window on Hans' side.

"I see a red door and I want to paint it black…"

She never had Hans down as a Stones fan, but there he was, tapping his fingers along.

She glanced out again at the crowds, normal people, doing normal things. Older generations sat on benches, younger ones zipping around on scooters, and the generations in between with push-chairs or beers in their hand; the two extremes of life.

Real lives.

"I look inside myself, and see my heart is black"

"I see my red door; I must have it painted black!"

She tried, for the briefest of moments, to picture herself sat in those crowds, amongst the normality of it all.

And then she thought about what she had done, was about to do, and how this would all end.

"Maybe then I'll fade away, and not have to face the facts…"

She could only see darkness…

"It's not easy facing up, when your whole world is black!"

And more death.

A lot would be lost, but at least one thing would come of it.

She would have done the right thing.

They pulled into Lars' driveway, fully, as there was no car occupying the space. Hildur had switched off while they had been talking over coffee, but one of the things that stuck in her mind was where he lived, opposite a park she remembered playing in all those years ago. Neither Hildur nor Hans moved, they just looked at what was before them. They didn't need to search the house.

A plastic storage unit was still half open, with spades and sandcastle buckets spilled out in front of the container, decorating the entrance. They had left in a hurry, probably due to the fickle nature of the weather, and the impending traffic. No discussion was had, Hildur put the car in reverse, backed out, and headed for the beach.

22

They Watched, and Waited

The two men kept within eyeshot of one another, one sitting, enjoying the view, the other reading. Both were doing as others did around them, nothing out of the ordinary. Nothing of any notable significance, while doing one thing of utmost importance: facing one another, and keeping their target within their sights at all times.

Lucas and Sven almost always operated as a pair. Maren liked consistency and familiarity when it came to operating, almost to the point of insisting upon it.

This was the pair's umpteenth assignment. It had become too many to count some time ago. They knew how the other worked, and rarely had to talk to be in-sync.

They worked as effortlessly as a slide: one acting as water, the other, gravity.

It all just flowed.

Joggers ran past in consistency, as well as the occasional bike, blocking the watching angles, but only momentarily.

They watched, and waited.

g before an opportunity presented itself. The
o was heading back up the path, towards the car
doubtedly something had been forgotten in the
rom of movement just moments before.

e man must have been good with words, as he appeared to
have reached an agreement with his wife to return to the car
alone, leaving her with both iPad addicts.

A shrewd man, gaining a little respite.

Respite, that would soon come at a cost.

The two men glanced at one another, and Lucas gave a signal.
Sven stood, and moved to intercept.

Lucas prepared himself, car key in hand. He traced the target,
and Sven, who disappeared behind a pack of joggers. Almost
time. He readied the syringe in his pocket, keeping it
concealed, but ready to go.

Lucas took one last glance back at his partner before he moved
in. A glance which didn't reveal much, except for one detail,
which sent a shockwave through him. He could no longer see
Sven.

He stood and tried to peer around to see where he was,
pedestrians intermittently blocking the view. And then, he saw
him. Only part of him, his foot, poking out on the ground from
behind a passer-by.

He froze at the sight, and went to take a step.

Although he tried, it didn't happen.

No sooner had he been paralysed by the sight of his
unconscious colleague, something else had rooted him to the
spot. He realised that his hand was up by his neck, but not by
his volition.

It was being gripped by someone else.

The only thing Lucas could manage, was to turn his head, just
enough to look at the face of the person who had plunged a
decent dose of Midazolam into his neck.

He stared, with gormless eyes. All he could make out before he
lost consciousness, were flashes of blonde hair poking out

82

from under a runner's cap, triumphant eyes, and a subtle smile, before he felt a sinking feeling, and the world became a black haze.

23

Concern Creeping In

'Oh my god! Is he OK?' asked a passer-by, who then changed his direction and walked over. A few joggers and dog walkers had gathered around within seconds of him hitting the ground, which was to be expected, it's what she said next that would be important.

The man had spoken in Icelandic, so Hildur clawed into the deep recesses of her memory, and replied in the same tongue.

'I'm not sure, he just fell as I passed, and I caught him,' Hildur replied, stumbling on a few words, with one hand sliding into her pocket, hiding the syringe.

She kept her head tilted forwards, looking down at Lucas, the peak of the cap covering most of her face, just in case the concerned man happened to be good at memorizing faces.

One of the gathered shouted for an ambulance to be called, which was Hildur's cue to get going.

'Well, it's lucky you caught him, he could have hit his head,' the man continued. 'I saw just as he fell, and I wondered... why you had your hand around his neck?' he said with a tone of intonation at the end, half resembling a question.

The man looked a little unsure, with a look of concern creeping into his expression.

'I just reacted on instinct, I didn't really think,' Hildur replied with a friendly smile, now remembering more of the language, as if not having walked for some time. It wasn't quite the same as slipping into your everyday shoes, something more akin to a lesser-used running shoe, awkward, but easing with each step. 'I hope he's okay though.'

The man's expression eased.

'And a good thing too,' he replied, now smiling back.

Hildur heard some growing voices and more commotion over the man's shoulder, where Sven lay. One unconscious man could be explained as coincidence, but two?

It was definitely time to get going.

'Well, this may sound strange, but I was on for a record 5km run. You can stay with him until help arrives, right?'

Hildur was suddenly aware she wasn't really dressed for it, and hoped the man was more preoccupied with looking at the body on the floor.

'Sure, there's plenty of us here now,' the man assured her as more people gathered the scene.

Time to exit.

Hildur stood and jogged off before the crowds got any larger, circling back around to the car park.

As she neared the car, she saw Hans – also sporting a new sports cap – stood with Lars, who looked to be in some shock.

His wife looked more confused than anything, and the addicts had peeled the iPads away from their eyes for the first time. It was real-life action, after all.

Hans had worked swiftly, taking out Sven, and then gathering Lars' wife and kids to safety.

After this commotion, they needed to leave, and fast.

The whole thing lasted less than thirty seconds, from the first body hitting the floor, to the second body down and the family gathered up and ready to go.

Lucas and Sven were good at what they did; Hildur and Hans were better.

Hildur walked over to them, whilst gathering thoughts on what to say.

A lot of explaining to do.

24

Vivid Clarity

The silence in the car actually lasted a little longer than Hildur thought it would, a welcome pause from the recent tumult.
But, as with all things, it came to an end.

'So... my family is in danger, because my husband ran you over?' Thorrun asked, somewhat rhetorically.
The explanations that had been given moments before – accurately, and in detail – had failed to set in. People in shock often failed to comprehend the most basic things, unless otherwise trained. It was a common weakness of the human mind.
Hildur reminded herself she was once like that too, and prepared herself for the conversation once more.

'Not entirely, no,' Hildur said gently, being patient. 'It's the fact that Lars found things on me after that he shouldn't have seen. They don't want anything potentially compromising coming back to them,'
One of the kids fidgeted and started to ask questions, and Lars shushed them.

'OK, well Lars won't say anything to anyone, will you?' Thorrun said as she looked at Lars.

'Of cours—'

'We trust that he wouldn't,' Hildur said, cutting Lars off, 'but they won't. That's not how they work. These people, they like to remain hidden, and will do anything to keep it that way. '

'So, we go to the police. They will sort this, I'm sure – '

'It won't work,' Hans interjected, 'The people we work fo... *worked* for, cannot be dealt with by local police. Higher powers in Norway and Sweden have gotten in their way and disappeared, I doubt your police force here would fare any better. They have influence everywhere.'

More silence followed. If it weren't for the mild rumble of the engine, Hildur swore she would have been able to hear the thoughts being processed, heavy and contemplative.

'So... what happens now?' asked the shaken mother, hesitantly.

'Now, we get you somewhere safe, until Hans and I sort this out here. Then we will get you away from here, away from the capital at least. Until we know it's safe to return.'

More silence ensued, but it felt frightful.

Hildur added some extra reassurance.

'This will blow over. These people, they will pay. And you will return to your normal life once they are gone.'

'These people? Aren't you one of them?'

Hildur searched for an answer, as Hans gave one.

'It's complicated. We were, but... let's just say that we have our differences now.'

Hans' final input seemed to satisfy their questions; for now. Either out of reassurance, or some lingering shock. Perhaps a bit of both. Either way, things were calmer for now.

Hildur focused back on the road and drove on, putting distance between them and the incident, running through ideas and places to take them where they wouldn't be found. She needed somewhere hidden where they wouldn't be spotted by any of TESS' operatives, and somewhere close by so that she could get to them quickly if needed, for a quick escape, or if they were found.

There weren't many places, but she narrowed it down to a few.

Before she finished laying out all options, one of them presented itself in bright, vivid clarity, 24-megapixel definition. Her phone flashed and buzzed next to her, illuminated with the caller ID.

Maren.

25

Loosen The Hold

Hildur clicked on the call, and pressed it to her ear. The same as before, she waited.

And for the second time, the caller spoke first.

'So, I'm guessing you either turned down my offer and headed south, or my two guys have mysteriously fallen down dead somewhere and won't answer me?... Am I close?' Maren asked.

'Nothing mysterious about it. It was in broad daylight.'

'Funny.'

A heavy sigh was followed by a small pause.

'He called, as you probably would have guessed,' Maren said. 'I didn't update him on everything. At this moment, he thinks you and Hans didn't make it out. He's waiting for me to confirm.'

Maren waited for a response, and Hildur waited for Maren to continue.

'I could still tell him otherwise, you know. You two could get out and disappear from this, start fresh somewhere. It doesn't have to be like this.'

'Oh, but it does, Maren. Going for me and Hans is one thing, we've both done shitty things and have to accept our fate whenever it comes our way. But an innocent family?'

Maren went to say something, but it came out as an incoherent noise as she was cut off.

'That's crossing a fucking line. You may not have ordered it, but you relayed the order. You were part of it.'

'Yes,' Maren admitted, 'and I don't deny it. As you said, we are in this game, and it makes us do difficult things. You really think I could say no to him and go against his order?'

'You could have at least tried to be creative, like you are now for us. Or perhaps offer us a way out *before* you tried to kill us?'

Silence held the line as some thought was given to the question.

'Better late than never?' Maren suggested, sarcastically.

'Funny.'

They both stopped at the stalemate of words, and paused a few moments.

'The offer stands, Hildur, to both of you. But it has to be taken now, this is a one-time offer just between you and me. If anyone else knows you are alive, then I can't do anything.'

'And the family?'

Hildur felt all eyes in the car turn to her, rooting her to the seat.

'I can't change that, you know I can't,'

'Can't, or won't?'

'Can't,' Maren replied, 'the whole of TESS has the order to bring them in, not just me, and they won't stop until they do,'

'Well then... fuck you, and your offer. If you won't stand up to him, then I will. He tried to kill me, Hans, and an innocent family. I'm not going to just slide away into nothing and hide. I'm going to make him pay, and anyone who stands in the way,'

'Hildur, if you just...'

Hildur blocked out Maren's words, and focused on the background noise of the call. She started to notice some distinguishable sounds, of people talking in what seemed large groups, crowds, and cars. Probably downtown.

Lots of voices, all in English, with an amalgam of mixed accents.

Tourists, almost definitely downtown.

'...If it has to be, then I guess...' Maren continued.

Hildur suppressed Maren's voice again, and listened to the others. The voices died away, and became less clustered and frenetic. One stood out more than the others: monologuing, akin to a history lesson.

Or a tour guide, giving a talk.

Hildur filtered out the other sounds, and reduced them to a low buzz.

She heard one word with particular clarity. "Leif."

Leif Erikson, who had a statue downtown, right outside the church.

'Hilly? Still there?'

'You know I hate that name.'

'I know,' her Handler admitted, and continued, 'so, we're just going to play cat and mouse around this small town until one finds the other?'

The background noise had completely faded away now. The sound had instantly dampened – like when you walk into a large room. Now Hildur was almost positive. And she had the upper hand again. Personal and local knowledge always trumped two day old operational knowledge and recon.

'No, no more chasing. I'm done with it. Only finishing things now. And this isn't a small town, it's a city. My city. And I'm going to get all of you out of it.'

Hildur noticed she was gripping the phone tighter than before, almost to the point of it shooting out of her grip. She found herself unable to loosen the hold.

'You came for an innocent family in my city, and now, I am coming for you.'

She didn't get a response, because she didn't allow time for one.

She hung up, took a long overdue breath, and headed for the church.

26

She Had To

In just under five minutes, three turns, and two red lights ran, Hildur stood one step away from the opening of the church. Hans had taken the car to find somewhere to park a few roads away, out of sight.

Hildur stepped in, glancing all around, checking corners and the upper seating area. No sign of the team, or her lapdog Jakob.

And no Maren.

She continued through, advancing towards the pulpit of the church.

Still nothing.

Maybe it wasn't the church?

She neared the end of the walkway, and as she did, saw a familiar throw of hair, and the usual look of a mobile phone attached to the side of the head.

Hildur came around the front, right into her eye-line, and, as she did, her Handler slowly lowered the phone. A small expression of surprise, but not much. She had been around long enough to experience bigger shocks. She took it in her stride.

They held the stare, as Hildur took a seat opposite, never breaking eye-contact.

The atmosphere inside felt freighted.

Maren gave a tiny smirk.

'You remember this place well then?'

'Of course.'

Her Handler shifted in her seat, but not so much as to look uncomfortable. Then she asked, 'So, what gave me away?'

'If there's one thing you can count on from loud and obnoxious tourists is for them to be loud and obnoxious.'

'Ah...' her Handler replied, trying desperately to hide her annoyance beneath a fake smile.

Hildur's glare remained fixed on her, and what had almost become a smile, faded from Maren's face.

'He won't stop, Hildur. If you keep doing this, it will only end one way. TESS has infinitely more man-power and resources than you do. You're alone. They'll keep going until they get you. Until he gets you'

Not so alone, Hildur thought.

'Then let him keep coming. He can try. And by my reckoning, he has lost men here already. I made sure of that. There can't be many left, not as many as he would like or need to deal with me anyway.'

'He'll bring reinforcements. He already has, they are on the way. I told you to leave while you had the chance.'

'I'll be long gone by the time they get here.'

'And how are you planning to leave? You don't think they are watching the airports? They've been over them from the start, in case this business with Fenrir went south.'

'I'll find a way.'

She knew she would. She had to.

Her Handler's expression shifted to something Hildur couldn't quite place, and said, 'I'm not sure what you're planning with me, but...' her eyes dropped momentarily, then locked back on Hildur's.

'Remember all those favourable exercises I put you on through the years? Most of the others had it much worse,'

98

'And a shame, too. I like a challenge.'

Maren reconsidered for a moment.

'And when your mother died, I looked out for you through that; Hekla, she was a wonderful woman, Hildur. Your Father wasn't exactly helpful to you then—'

'Stop. I don't want to hear it. I didn't ask for any of that.'

'I know; I wanted to do it, to help you. And I still do. Please don't—'

'My mind is made up, Maren.'

'So, why take so long about this and listen to me?'

'Waiting,' Hildur replied, as she stood.

'Waiting? Waiting for what?'

As she finished asking, Hildur began to walk away towards the aisle.

Maren remained open-mouthed, wanting to ask again but not daring to. Her sense of relief silenced her, as she eased her grip from the edge of her seat for the first time in two minutes. Her hands were stiff and numb.

Her plea to be spared had been listened to.

She watched Hildur walk away, slumped back into the chair and tilted her head back, letting out a sigh.

As the breath left her, Hans' fingers slithered around the front of her throat from behind, locking together in a vice, and squeezed.

27

Protectors Now

After grabbing some essentials from the family's home – mainly chargers for electricals – they all crammed into the car and headed East. Lars and Thorrun had been told the plan, and hadn't said much in response to it, neither had much say in the matter. They were at the whim of their protectors now.

Hildur and Hans were taking them to their cabin, a summer house in a remote location, far from the city and untraceable, due to it being in another family member's name. It was about as safe as they could get them for now.

It was a long stretch of driving, especially with two young kids in the car, which made the 5 hours feel something more approximating double. Lars and Thorrun took it in turns to try to hush or distract them, which Hildur appreciated.

Hans tried to engage in small talk with them, probably out of boredom and frustration at not knowing Icelandic, but Hildur saved them from it by directing Hans into a conversation about the drone strike, and what his favourite forms of incendiary were.

It kept him busy for a good twenty minutes.

Too easy.

Thankfully for all involved in the journey, Hans' attempts at small talk stopped. He and Hildur switched at the wheel while the family took naps. Hildur found herself at the wheel, for the first time in a long time, alone. She drank in the feeling, along with the midnight sun, and continued along the empty road.

*

The drop-off was a fast ordeal, which was no surprise, given what had happened. Although getting them involved was due to her, it had also been out of her control, but she had got them out of harm's way.

Lars did most of the talking, and Hildur gave him instructions not to leave for several days. She would give them a signal when it was ok to do so.

Maybe somewhere in Thorrun's silence there was some appreciation of what they had done for the... she hoped.

Hildur and Hans made their way back to the car, and rolled away from the remote cabin. Small in its size, and becoming smaller by the second she viewed it in the rear-view mirror. The sight of it shrank, but the apprehension grew deep inside of her: *what if*? What if they do find them somehow?

She couldn't take them with her. And she also couldn't stay.

It was the best of a bad bunch of options.

She hated not having better options.

Hans interrupted her thoughts with the same concerns.

'Likelihood they get found?' Hans asked, much to Hildur's annoyance.

'Can't and don't want to think about it, Hans. We've done the best we can.'

'We could have taken them with us.'

'We have no idea what we'll encounter on the way out of here, and we can't operate fully with them around. TESS has lost people, but Maren said that more have been sent. We don't know how many, we have to expect the worst.'

Hans looked at Hildur for a few seconds while she drove, and then looked away.

She wasn't entirely sure what kind of look it was, but she could guess. He didn't fully agree with it, that much was clear. And in all honesty, neither did she.

Hildur didn't engage with him anymore, nor with her thoughts. She just looked on ahead at the barren stretch before them, trying to remember what darkness looked like.

28

The Man Of Silence

Jakob's hand shook while holding the phone to his ear. Although all too aware of it, trying to steady it didn't work. He would have maybe felt some shame, if it weren't for who was about to be on the other end of the call. Most were uneasy when speaking with him, some frightened. Particularly when delivering bad news. A part of him began to will the other end of the line not to pick up; to hear a beep and to be returned to the home screen. Then reality kicked back in with a click.

Silence from the other end.

The nervous caller spoke first.

'S… Sir?… Umm…' The silence felt judgemental, like he could feel him staring at him through the phone. He may as well have been in the backseat, breathing down his neck. He swallowed with difficulty, and continued.

'She… she got to her. We don't know how. She left her body in the church.'

He desperately wanted to add the next bit he was expecting – *'Where she was now'* – but he couldn't. Instead, the silence returned with a weight.

He could hear the man on the other end breathe.

Heavily.

Menacingly.

The nerves of the caller got the better of him again, and added, 'But, we did get a report of a family accompanied by a man and a woman, heading out of town in the last hour. Heading East. The description of the man was similar to Hans. He could still be alive. If it is them, they could be heading to the port out there. We did some digging, and found there is just one ferry port out there. They might have guessed we are watching the airports.'

He stopped, finally, pleased with what he had offered.

The man of silence, finally spoke.

'So, you called me, to tell me that more of my team are dead, where they *might* be, and a ferry timetable?'

It was delivered at a slow pace and in a hushed tone, but was anything but calm.

A flat rage simmered and seethed beneath the words.

Jakob's eyes went wide, the man's words having delivered an imaginary gun, pointing straight at him. He could feel the crosshairs, aiming right between his eyes. He tried to take a breath, but his body didn't listen.

The man continued.

'Do you know what I will do to you, to all of you, if you do not track them down and let them escape?'

Although rhetorical, Jakob felt the urge to answer. Nodding at first, and his senses returning, he remembered words were needed.

'Y...Yes, Sir.'

'I want them both dead by the end of the day, and the family dealt with. You stay there and deal with Maren's body. Send the rest of the team after them.'

The man spoke no further, and left a now breathless and perspiring caller alone in the car, with nothing but sweaty palms and a dead dial tone.

29

'Yeah, I'm Ready'

They pulled in at a service station, having let the needle get a little too close to the red than was comfortable for either of them, and, as much as Hans protested, Hildur didn't quite agree that they themselves needed refuelling just as much as the car. Ever since SERE training in some of the most remote mountains in the world, hunting and being hunted by wild animals, Hildur had reclassified what the definition of '*starving*' was.

Hans, juggling stacks of sweets and snacks, had other ideas.

Hildur browsed a few of the aisles, scanning items, but not really looking at anything. Her focus was elsewhere. She couldn't think about food right now.

She left Hans to his feeding-frenzy and headed outside.

It was peaceful.

Still.

A distant hum carried itself across the vast, empty expanse, uninterrupted.

It could have been in the next town, or at the end of the island.

It felt as though she could hear right through to the other side of the land.

A perfect silence.

It was cut short by the high-pitch chime of the door opening, probably from Hans spilling through the door with his pile of snacks.

Although upon turning around, she saw not Hans, but a mother and daughter, carrying their own moderately sized shopping.

The daughter had approached Hildur before Hildur had realised.

She was still in a pensive trance.

Maybe from the hypnotic tranquil landscape; maybe from lack of sleep.

Whichever it was, she was snapped out of it by the little girl holding something out to her.

Hildur looked down at the chocolate bar, and something whirred in the back of her mind: a memory trying to present itself. She had seen it before, a long time ago, although it was different now, she remembered it.

As if learning for the first time, she found herself looking at what had been her favourite snack as a child.

How could something once held so dear barely register as a memory?

Hildur still hadn't spoken, but the girl did.

'Here ya go, Miss. You did'n get anythin' in the shop. You looked hungry.'

Hildur woke up sometime around the word '*shop*', and, as she took the bar, she finally found some words.

Kind of.

'Th... thank you. That's... that's really kind of you,' she said smiling, first at the girl, and then to the mother. She was around Hildur's age, and their appearances were somewhat similar.

The mother returned with a kind '*you're welcome*' smile, but didn't verbalise it.

She ushered the kid into the car, and they pulled away.

Hans finally appeared, carrying more than one man would ever need, and half of his own bodyweight in snacks, and made it to Hildur, miraculously without dropping any of it.

He said something, but it didn't really register.

Hildur watched the child in the car, smiling, holding a bunny rabbit cuddly toy up in the air, as they mouthed something to it, probably speaking on its behalf, playing the role of 'Mr. Rabbit', in full-force and with maximum commitment, as kids did.

Imagination and innocence at its fullest.

Hans said something again, which brought her focus back now. And a third time.

'Hildur! Hello?'

'What did you say?'

'Jeez Hilly, I said are you ready to go?'

Hildur looked back at the car, which had pulled out onto the main road and was on its way to becoming a visual speck, and a memory.

She turned back to Hans.

'Yeah. I'm ready.'

30

Watch The Road

They drove past mini glaciers and lakes of ice, and began their descent down through the fjord, flanked either side by vast, slanted mountains that looked to be falling back into the land itself, staggered with lines worn by time, ice ages having left their mark.

The road was steep and winding, snaking its way down to ground level, eventually reaching down to a solitary small town at the coast, where a mere 50 houses or so stood. It was as close to the quintessence of remoteness as you could get without actually being an island.

The fjord was shut off from the rest of the world for up to six months of the year, and the sun's rays touched it for just three. One treacherous mountain pass gave access in and out, and that was it.

Unforgiving.

The only other option was the open expanse of the Atlantic that lay on the other side of the town. Being summer, they didn't face such obstacles. Hans knew nothing of this, but Hildur did, and she counted her blessings for it.

They made the short drive though the town – all of two minutes – and parked up outside the ferry port. Hans went in while Hildur stayed on guard, scanning the scant few cars that did go by. It was a sleepy town even on a summer's day such as this.

Hans returned fairly swiftly holding two tickets in hand, but not looking pleased. He climbed back into the car, threw them onto the dashboard, and let out a huff.

'Well, mainly good news. There were tickets left for today, and there is one more departure. Bad news...we have to wait for two hours.'

Hildur took a moment to deal with the dread. She wanted to get on the move and away from there as fast as possible.

No more risks.

'We should hide out, somewhere with a good view of the road, just until we are ready to leave,' Hildur suggested.

'It's just two hours Hilly, I'm sure it'll be fine. We didn't pick up a tail, we would have seen.'

'I don't think it's unreasonable for them to have guessed we have come here. And if they did, they would be just an hour or so behind. He would have given the order not long after we left the beach, if he did make that assumption. It's a small chance, but a chance all the same. And I don't want to take any more to add to it.'

Hans went to reply, but caught himself at the sight of Hildur's severity.

He considered it for a moment, sided with her and with caution, and agreed.

'OK. We watch the road.

31

Completely Still

A little over an hour had passed, and some 40 cars had gone by. Among them, only a few had had potential. Some were removed on the count of there being a child present in the car, and the others – although having passengers that would match the appearance of TESS' operatives – were also removed as a threat due to them either having a car being far too old, or the passengers looking far too relaxed and unfocused.

Given the severity of the situation for them, and the time constraints, it seemed highly improbable.

Their lives were on the line too.

Hans and Hildur sat in their car on the side of the road, in between a smattering of other vehicles left vacant by the day's hikers. They had a good view of the road, as it twisted and wound down the valley. The view was partially cut off as it snaked around a waterfall on the other side of the road, before coming into view again, just as cars levelled with them and passed. Hildur used the moments in between to stare into the cascade, focusing on one central spot, until it seemed that it wasn't actually moving at all. It stood still, and all things around it.

Completely still.
And then Hans' words made it move again.

'Ferry ETA 75 minutes,' Hans stated, snapping her back to the car.
'We could call it quits soon.'
Hildur ran calculations and timings. If they were to get on the ferry now, it would leave a window of an hour for them to make it to the fjord – if they were on the way – and board, leaving them trapped on the ferry together.
Potentially outnumbered and almost definitely outgunned.
There would also be some security on the ship, and civilian witnesses.
The only escape route would be an icy and deathly plunge into the Atlantic.
Even if they somehow went unnoticed on the journey, there would be no easy escape at the other end. TESS would have more people waiting on arrival.
They couldn't risk that death trap.
They had to wait until the last possible moment to board.

'Not yet,' Hildur said. 'We can't risk it. If they made it on there with us and got a visual, they'd get back up on our arrival when we dock... we just can't. It'd be all over. All of this would have been for nothing. Just because we didn't want to wait a little longer.'
'OK! OK, Hilly. If it'll really put you at ease, we'll wait.

For all his bravado and ego, he had a nice side really. Hildur had never spent much time with him to really notice, only in training where she saw the competitive side of him.
She liked this new side more.
She felt herself slipping into a smile, and restrained it quickly.
At least she thought she did.

'When we're outta this Hilly, I'm gonna take you on one of my meditation hikes.'

Hildur physically craned her neck around to look straight at him, disbelief across her face. This, she could not hide.

Meditation? Hans?!

Hans laughed at the look.

'I know! Not really me is it? Something I've been trying recently. Well not so much meditation, more mindfulness I think they call it. But it's good. Might help you relax a little more when you need to.'

She remained staring at him in shock, Hans still smiling at her.

'Sure,' Hildur replied. 'I'd like that.'

Hans changed the tone, and asked, 'Hildur, what happened, really?'

Hildur shifted at the words, becoming visually uncomfortable.

'I mean, that guy, Lars? He found your weapon on you. I get it, it's not good. But did it really warrant TESS trying to kill us for it? All of us? It doesn't seem right.'

The question forced Hildur to see the memory again.

Needle up high, ready, waiting....but...Hildur wasn't sure how long she had been staring at the woman; however long it had been, it was too long.

This should be finished by now.

The woman didn't move, and just stared at Hildur.

"Please... please let me live,"

Hildur couldn't, she had to carry this out. But... how could she now? With what was before her?

She couldn't take her eyes off it...

The moment was interrupted by an approaching car, which was cut from view by the ledge. They both focused on the spot waiting for it to reappear, and as it did, all the tell-tale signs along with it: 4x4 SUV, three males, no kids, expressions of focus, and to top it all off, a big *'I'm not from around here!'* rental sticker plastered on the back screen as it passed.

Hans and Hildur shared a short glance with one another, and fired up the engine. A few seconds later, they pulled onto the road, once again one step ahead of their pursuers.

32

Follow Them

No more than a minute passed before they reached the edge of the town, and they were faced with an immediate decision – turn left or right, to stay directly on their tail, or to travel on the parallel street and hope they could maintain visual enough of the time. To tail them directly would soon become suspicious in such a small place, so they would have to be cautious and be prepared to peel off at any time, which ran the risk of losing them. They decided to split up.

Hans would continue to tail them in the car, and Hildur would take a vantage point up in the town's church. It had blind spots, but, most importantly, it had a view of the port.

After the car in front had turned left, Hans and Hildur followed them down the first stretch of road, until they reached the church. Hans pulled over, and Hildur jumped out into the church car park, hidden from view. She closed the door, and Hans sped off to get back on the trail, and Hildur entered the church.

It had been quiet outside, but that now seemed noisy in contrast to inside the chapel. The door had marked her arrival with a notable thud that echoed and bounced around the walls.

By the time it finished reverberating and got back to where it had started, she realised she was alone.

Walking into the nave of the church, some ten strides bringing her almost to the altar at the front, she turned back to look at the hundred or so seats. Up above, a small organ sat on the upper viewing deck, as a perfect centrepiece. The acoustics would be every pianist's dream while playing to the masses.

She headed up the steps, and walked along to the bell tower. With just about enough room, she manoeuvred around it to get to the outward-facing side, with a view of the town. After a few moments of scanning the roads, she soon saw a black 4x4, being cautiously followed by Hans.

33

The Right Balance

Hans applied the brakes on and off, making sure not to get too close; there was nothing quite like a tailgater to draw the attention of a driver.

A car behind him urged him forwards, but he found the right balance.

The Jeep in front slowed a few times, checking corners and side roads, scanning for them, before moving on again. Three turns and three roads in, they approached the fourth, which threw up a problem. It was going to bring them back on themselves, leaving Hans with a decision: to continue and risk suspicion, or to break off and hope Hildur had eyes on them?

Hans ran it through, weighing up the options. It was possible they were lost, or just roaming aimlessly, searching. It was also possible that they knew they were turning back on themselves, and they had become aware of the same car behind them, and it was a test.

Which was too risky.

The rental eventually pulled forward, turning left, rolling slowly forward down the road. *Maybe searching.*
Maybe testing.
Hans pulled forward, and turned right.
With no more watching to do, he found the next vacant driveway and parked up, reached for his phone, and called Hildur.
Phone already in hand, she picked up after one ring.

'I've had to pull back, they were going in circles, couldn't risk it. Please say you have eyes on?'
'Hang on,' Hildur said.
She searched up ahead, by the lake, and a road next to the school.
Nothing.
Every road was chopped into tiny visual segments, due to a cluster of shops and restaurants in front of the church.
'Hildur? Any luck?'
'Not yet.'
Then she searched farther ahead, to the edge of the town where it met the coast. She saw the ferry pulling into the port, and a black SUV pulling into the car park.

'Hilly?'
'Yes. Got 'em.'
Hans waited.
'They're at the ferry port, heading into the ticket office.'
'Shit.'

34

All It Comes Down To

Hildur clicked off the call, and watched the men as they entered the port. Two of them made their way into the ticket office, while the third stood outside by the car, on watch.

It would probably take all of twenty seconds for them to ask the staff member if they had seen anyone matching their description in the last two hours, how many tickets he had purchased, and the destination.

Child's play.

They reappeared thirty seconds later, stood and spoke for a few moments, one of them pointing back towards the town, and then they all entered the car.

They knew.

She didn't call Hans right away, she needed to think.

Hildur looked around at her surrounding: scanning the lake, out to the ocean, and the mountains.

Thinking.

Blocked going forwards.

Blocked going back.

And can't stay put.

Leaving only one option: to go through them.

Being outnumbered was never ideal, but you rarely ever got to choose your ideal.

They still had the advantage of time on their side, albeit a small advantage. They could choose where and when this would happen, which was something that presented its own potential.

And they had to use what they had.

She continued to gaze out, at the stretch of ocean leading to freedom, wondering if they would make it out there. Still, it wasn't a bad place to slow down and think. It was probably the calmest place she had been to have a real chance to plan, and one of the last places she expected to be interrupted.

'Imagining, is the first step,' a voice said from behind. Hildur had spun around by the time the sentence was finished.

'All the remaining steps, lay in the execution.'

The spoken words had been delivered by a diminutive man well north of his seventies, wearing a warm smile, piercing blue eyes, and white robes.

The priest.

Hildur wasn't quite sure how to respond, so instead explained the reason for her being up in the bell tower.

'I needed somewhere quiet to think.'

It was less effort to speak Icelandic this time, it just came naturally. No more stumbling, just easy and comfy steps.

Like running shoes.

'In this little town, you felt the need to come up here? It must be one tough predicament you face.'

You don't know the half of it.

'You could say that,' Hildur replied.

The priest considered her for a moment.

'No matter how bad it may seem, there are always fates far worse. Take death: most people think it is this itself.'

'Yeah, that's a pretty bad one,' Hildur said, casting an eye back out towards the port, checking their progress. They hadn't moved.

Yet.

'Yes, it is, but far from the worst. It depends on the timing,' the priest said, smiling.

Hildur waited for him to continue.

'Take someone in their youth, at a good point in their life. It's seen as a tragedy: bad timing. Or, when they are much older, perhaps even in pain. They may even welcome it, a release. A relief to themselves, and all around them. It is still the same person, only a different time.'

'Why mention time so often?' Hildur asked.

'Well, that is all it comes down to, isn't it?'

Hildur just looked at him, unsure of what to say.

'We all go eventually, and none of us make it out in the end. It is just a matter of, '*when*?' And '*when*' is a matter of time. Which really leaves only one question: how should we spend that time? What shall we do with it while we are here?'

Hildur didn't say anything. Not that she wanted to anyway, she just let the words settle on her.

'Let perspective guide you,' the priest added, as Hildur turned to look outward again, no longer looking for their pursuers, but for a response to all of this.

She had to concede, he did have a point.

Worse things happen at sea.

Hildur turned back to reply, and as she did, she found herself overlooking the empty nave of the church below, but no priest.

How long had she been thinking?

Before she started questioning her sanity – which she was tempted to do – she had to make a call first, before the inspiration left her.

With no more than two rings, Hans answered, barely getting his question out, of "*any developments?*" when Hildur spoke over him.

'We go to them. We take control,' she said.

'O...kay. What you thinking?'

'We let them see us, then lead them away from here.'

'Where?'

Hildur glanced upwards, up high to the left, into a cut inside of the mountain.

'We lead them up the mountainside, high up, and way from here. We pick our battleground, while we still have the chance.'

She paused.

'While we still have time.'

35

We Go Through Them

After Hildur finished laying out the plan, she hung up and made her way down and through the church, and waited inside the front door until Hans arrived.

She scanned around on the way, to see if she could see the priest. There was a quiet couple, reading a text, and another solitary figure looking to a statue for answers.

But no sign of the man she had spoken with.

She peered through the door, and saw Hans approaching down the road. She waited a few moments, stepped out, and got in alongside him.

'Are you sure about this?' Hans asked.

'Yeah. We go through them; it's a great opportunity. We do this our way.'

Hans' expression didn't agree with Hildur's words.

'I'm not sure about that.'

'Depends how you look at it, I guess.' Hildur said.

They drove another full stretch of road before talking again.

'And you're sure about when we get up there?'

'Hans…'

Hildur looked at him.

'Stop. I said I'm ok with it. I wouldn't suggest it otherwise.'

They approached the port, now just one road away. Having pulled over to avoid being seen, Hildur climbed out and went on foot. She disappeared in between two houses, keeping wide of the port, using other boats as cover. She hopped from one to another, trying to get a clear sight of the port. To see the SUV.

Hans waited in the car, tapping away on the wheel. He didn't like waiting. He preferred skipping straight to the doing. Always.

Hildur reappeared some minutes later, and returned to the car. She looked calm.
'See 'em?'
She was still smiling.
Hans' words slowly filtering in. Drip by drip.
'Yeah, they're there. Parked to the left of the office, watching and waiting. Sitting ducks.'
'Well then...' Hans began. 'Let's go get 'em!'

36

An Easy Catch

After arguing about who would wait at the car while the others carried out reconnaissance on the nearby buildings, rank was soon pulled, and the argument won. The two longer-standing henchmen went for the walk, leaving the less experienced Seb by himself.

Still annoyed, and the short straw acting as a chip on his shoulder, Seb thumbed away at his phone, glancing up every now and then at any sign of movement, which wasn't often. There wasn't a lot of movement anywhere in this town.

He wondered how people could live in such a small place and not go crazy, mainly out of lack of things to do, but also out of the paucity of Tinder options.

He flicked through a little more, regretted swiping no to what turned out to be the last choice, and then ran out of options.

He always got bored with these kinds of missions. Lots of waiting around and watching, but not much action.

He was dying for some action.

He took a rare pause from his phone to watch the road, and a good thing he did too. With a car rolling round the corner, he found himself looking directly at two people through the windscreen, them looking back at him. Two seconds passed, before they turned around and sped off.

Got 'em! What an easy catch.

Another second passed as all of this processed, before he hopped in the Jeep, and drove to where his colleagues were, horn blaring.

Seconds later, Axel and Kristjan came flying out, scanning in panic, realising what was happening, and then rushed to the SUV.

'Get in! They're here. Just drove off down that road,' Seb spilled out as he frantically pointed and gestured.

'Switch,' Axel demanded as he moved to climb into the driver's seat.

'But I—' Seb began, before he was interrupted with a word spoken as sternly as the stare that was given with it.

'Now.'

Seb spoke no more and switched with Axel, and with Kristjan occupying the passenger seat, he shuffled to the back, a perfect visual setup of their rank-order.

They turned onto the road, and soon saw their target at the far end of the long stretch of road leading to the mountain pass.

'We've got 'em,' Kristjan said confidently, and with a smile.

'How's that?' Seb asked from the back.

'Because that road leads to one town only, a town where we have people waiting. Let's give 'em a call for a heads u—'

Kristjan paused bringing the phone to his ear, holding it uselessly in the air. None of them spoke, as they watched the car up ahead turn off a side road, and head up a steep road towards the mountain side.

'Idiots,' Axel said smiling, no longer able to hide his excitement as he squeezed the steering.

'Now they are really trapped.'

37

Safe Now

It was exciting having real life police in the house, not like in the games or movies. They were actually here, with their uniforms and guns! It was so exciting that Fannar had put his iPad down for more than a minute to watch what was happening.

Bryndis on the other hand wasn't so taken, and had returned back to her screen moments after their arrival.

One of the policemen seemed to be the main leader, the captain, like Captain America or something. He took charge and did a lot of talking. Lots. Of. Talking.

Adults sure did talk a lot.

Fannar heard his mother crying, and she rushed around, picking up things and packing them into a bag. His father was listening, and talking.

More talking.

Bryndis nudged him on the arm, causing him to slip his finger from the screen.

High-score lost.

Damn it!

'Bryndis!' Fannar yelled.
'Quiet you two!' Lars shouted.

Fannar sank back down into the depths of the sofa.
Fine, start again.
New mission.
Level One.
Pow! pow! pow!
Thorrun came over, juggling bags, tears gone, and gave orders.

'Come on you two, we're leaving,'
'But Mumma! I just started—'
'No!' she said sternly, 'you can finish it in the car,'
'Awwwwwww!' Fannar sounded.
'These policemen are going to take us back home where we will be safe now. It's over.'
Fannar gave in.
'OK, fine!'

Both kids got up and followed the grownups out, the lead policeman smiling at Fannar and ruffling his hair as he passed.
He saw the gun up close, and the hand-cuffs.
So cool.
Not quite as cool as those Angry Birds though!
They all climbed in the car, and pulled out of the gravel driveway, Bryndis and Fannar in the back.
Fannar moved the policeman's coat out of the way to get comfy.
Jet black, with a big shiny badge.
Awesome.
The iPads were back in hand within seconds, and the tapping began once more.
Right... start again.
New mission.
Level One.
Pow! Pow! Pow!

38

They've Bought It

It handled well, considering its age.

Apart from the odd wheel-spin here and there, the ageing and reluctant motor did what was asked of it. Hans checked the rear view mirror intermittently, checking the progress of their pursuers.

Hildur kept him updated, but he looked anyway.

Old habits.

'They've bought it,' Hildur announced. 'They're following.'

Focusing on the ascension and the bends, Hans was in a trance. A metre from the gravel path was a sheer drop, a possible event horizon of their journey. Hans wasn't going to let such a thing happen.

He stopped checking back and put full-focus on the path ahead.

Midway up the mountainside it levelled out, opening out to a rocky, moss-covered area that was – although still slanted – level enough to park the car.

And to fight.

'It's time,' Hildur began. 'Just like we said. We even out the playing field.'

*

Close to a minute later, the pursuers approached the slanted landscape, and Axel slowed, assessing the change of terrain. He did all the thinking, as he knew the other two wouldn't. And then he made his choice.

'Guns ready,' Axel ordered, pulling out his own.
'Can't even see 'em though,' Seb replied from the back.
Axel tried to hold back his irritation, but a heavy exhale still escaped him.
'Can you see gravity? Or hurricane force winds?'
'Whaa?'
The driver's irritation now came through in his mannerisms, throwing an arm up in the air and scrunching his face.
'Jesus! I know you can't be picky about last minute backup, but fuck me!'
The man in the back stayed quiet this time as a look of embarrassment settled on him.
Axel and Kristjan flicked off the safety, shortly followed by Seb, reluctantly drawing out his weapon, without any real conviction.

They drove through the gap cautiously, past what were now sizeable boulders, towering over their 4x4.
If one of them decided it was time to fall, they would be goners.
They slowed, almost to a complete stop, when they saw a car up ahead, stuck, with its rear raised up in the air, and smoke gently rising from the front.

'Stay with the car and watch our backs,' Axel ordered to Seb.
He accepted the order with silence.

The two men in front climbed out, spread wide, keeping sufficient distance from one another, as they approached the stranded car.

Axel stumbled on the uneven terrain.

'Careful on this ground,' Axel said, stabilising himself.

'Got it.'

Smoke continued to rise from the crashed car, as they drew closer and closer.

39

Even Out The Numbers

They advanced, weapons and gaze aimed steadily at the target, with the occasional glance to the ground to check their footing. Although mostly flat where they were, it quickly lost its consistency, becoming not only uneven, but scattered with crevices.

Some small enough to just lose balance, others large enough to be lost down.

Seb, who had been tasked with watching their blind spots, was doing so intently. No more Tinder scrolling or checking his phone. Finally, some action that he was waiting for.

His complete focus was on what was happening in front of him.

Possibly a little too much.

He gave no thought to what might be around him.

Or behind.

Hildur slipped out from behind a boulder, and made careful steps to position herself behind him.

Time to even out the numbers.

She slid her arms around his neck from behind, covered his mouth, and applied pressure all around. She made sure to catch him at the end of his exhale, to speed up the process. By catching him unawares, and on the exhale, she was able to get sufficient grip to press on his carotid artery, jugular vein, and to block the airway.

The carotid no longer supplied oxygen to the brain, the jugular could no longer let blood exit the brain, and no oxygen in the airway to help him last for a few seconds longer.

A deadly triumvirate.

As the air left him, so did his gun, dropping to the soft ground below.

The limp body soon followed it, laying side-by-side.

The men were now a few strides from the car up ahead.

Hildur climbed into the Jeep that they had kindly left open and running, and accelerated, the heads in front turning to the noise.

As the guns rose and took aim, Hildur lowered her head, and sped into them.

By the time they thought about taking a shot, it was too late.

They split, diving out of the way: one left, the other right.

Divided.

Before the impact of the cars' front and rear bumpers meeting, Hildur jumped out, immediately entering into a roll, and was up and charging at Axel, who was scrambling for his pistol.

He made it in time and gripped the handle, his finger sliding onto the trigger, and began to lift it up towards the target: Hildur's centre mass.

It didn't make it far, as it dropped down again, accompanied by a loud ringing in his ear. Deafening.

He was reacquainted with the ground once more, flopping onto his back, his head cushioned from the blow by the soft moss below.

Hildur's strike had sent him reeling, but no knockout. He went with the roll, and used its momentum to get himself distanced from Hildur, and to buy some time.

Now a few paces away, he tried to get on his feet.

He tried, but physics vetoed his effort.

Hildur closed the gap, ready to strike.

Axel's second attempt was more successful, as he eventually fought off gravity and staggered into something resembling an upright position.

Unsteady, but standing.

Hildur thought about keeping the pressure on and charging him, or to ease off and assess the situation more.

She chose to let him stand.

No need to rush while having the upper hand.

Axel had regained some composure, but not his full balance. He swayed on the spot, his hands in uneven positions. He tried his best to not show the discomfort in his expression, but the rest of his body didn't get the update.

Two contrasting looks: his lower half more telling of the truth, showing his vulnerability that he could not hide.

Hildur heard a grunt from the other side of the Jeep, and scuffling, before the sound of someone hitting the floor.

Come on Hans.

Hildur advanced forward, causing Axel to shift awkwardly.

She closed the gap, and was close to striking distance, as Axel lunged forwards, which was easily negated by a quick side-step from Hildur. It was a move of desperation from a fighter who knew they were injured. He was in panic mode, and like most fighters in panic, saw only the head, and forgot everything else.

He had lost his composure.

Atli's voice came to her, *"A quick low kick will take 'em by surprise, and they have to shift their weight to avoid it. Behind the knee to disarm; or the front for end-game."*

End game.

Hildur delighted in the crisp and calm breeze, her hands up to the side of her face, poised and ready.

Her breathing slow, and steady.

As sure as Hildur was it would come again, it did.

This time – after side-stepping a right-hook – Hildur sprang off of her back foot, sending all momentum towards Axel's knee-cap, which buckled instantly from the stomp-kick.

They tended to only like bending in one direction.

Axel's scream shattered the peace and quiet that had been present on the mountainside.

He stumbled back onto his one good leg with all of his weight, which trembled under the strain.

"Time it well, the weight on the leg will do most of the work for you."

His imposing size had its advantages in some fights, but with a busted kneecap it was a huge hindrance, each step causing considerable pain.

He was there for the taking.

Hildur went for the last uneasy leg, and swept it out from under him. As soon as his back hit the ground, with the Earth itself delivering a straight shot to his spine, another blow was delivered to his front – into his solar plexus – by Hildur's fist.

More air than the man knew he had, left him.

He tried desperately to suck some air in, but nothing came.

He wriggled and writhed, but to no avail. It didn't help, just a human instinct that he couldn't fight off.

He pawed uselessly at his throat, at the ground around him, towards the sky... and then he slowed, easing his arms down to his sides, until he lay as still and motionless as the ground beneath him.

40

The Darkness Below

Hildur rushed around the 4x4 towards the sound of the moans and grunts, gliding and hopping over and around the jagged and bumpy ground.

She found Hans on top and overpowering Kristjan, who soon stopped struggling, and gave in. Hans eased his grip and stood, and began to walk to Hildur, with a smirk that couldn't quite hold itself back.

'Nice one Hilly,' he said, with that awful, cheesy wink.

But it didn't bother her so much this time. Somehow it was comforting.

Reassuring.

There was nothing quite like a near death experience to put things into perspective.

Hildur couldn't help but smile this time. After all this, they were almost free. That was cause enough to let the little things go, even if they were a bit annoying.

Hildur realised she was beginning to lift her arms up as she neared him, getting ready for a hug.

She couldn't remember ever doing that.

She thought of stopping it, to fight off the moment of weakness. But Hans' smile spoke to something inside of her, and she stopped fighting it, and decided to let it happen.

She raised her open arms up to him.

'Next time I doubt you, just tell me to shu—'

Hildur found her smile drop, as Hans' face changed.

It contorted and tightened.

Hildur's smile completely disappeared now.

A look of pain and panic was now stricken across his face, as he clutched at his side, and wheezed out an unnatural breath that sent a chill through Hildur.

She looked to where his hand was grasping.

His hand was resting on a blade that was lodged into his ribs, being held by the previously presumed incapacitated Kristjan. He hadn't recovered enough to stand, just enough to support himself on one arm, and reach up with the other.

Hildur, still watching on in shock, told her body to move. She had been frozen still for some three seconds, but it felt closer to an hour; time just stood still.

She strode forward, put a boot to Kristjan's face, and put him down for good.

She turned to Hans, to grab onto him, but he had already dropped to his knees.

The facial expression hasn't changed much, still riddled with shock. Hildur dropped down with him in sync, placing her hands on either side of him. Hans dropped down farther still, and lay on his back.

Hildur tried to fight every action, to hold him upright, to lift him up, but it was no use.

'No. No...' Hildur's voice was flat and monotone from her attempt to not panic, but the emotion started to break through. 'Hans. You... You can't...'

'Hil... Hilly...' Hans fought the words out, each one leaving on the coat-tails of an exhale.

'Ss... stop. It... s... OK.'

But it wasn't OK, none of this was. They were at the finish line; they were so close.

He reached to his side again, towards the handle, which judging from its size, Hildur realised it was probably a sizeable blade too.

She didn't want to risk pulling it out just yet, in case it had punctured something that would accelerate the bleeding.

Hildur took off her outer shirt and used it to press around the entrance, to slow the bleeding until she thought of something better.

'It's OK Hans, I already have pressure on...'

He wasn't reaching for the wound.

He pulled out the two ferry tickets, and held them out to Hildur, shaking from expelling his last drop of energy.

She took them, as his hand immediately dropped back down again.

She stared at the tickets.

Then at him.

And then at the blood, pooling out from around her hands and shirt, as it raced down to the ground in a constant flow.

Red and green were now blended on the moss below in equal measures.

She couldn't find any more words.

Hildur raced through choices of what to do, never really stopping to think about any of them.

Rush to a doctor in the town?

Leave the blade in?

Take it out and try to fix him here?

RAM: Regain, control, and, and... move? No, no!

Fuck, FUCK!

The panic scrambled her attempt to make a choice.

Seconds later, Hans made it for her.

He raised his hand once more and placed it on her arm as gently as he looked at her, and smiled at her like he never had before.

They locked eyes for what felt like a day, as everything around them slowed and stood still, blacking out.

He looked not *at* her, but *through* her.

He could see her.

141

Hans' smile faded as he closed his eyes, and his arm fell from her as he sunk down, all energy leaving him as he settled into the ground.

Only the remnants of a smile remained.

Hildur continued to stare at him, just watching the stillness and the calm. No more thoughts came to her, everything just stopped.

She moved her hand away from the bloodied shirt, and let it slide to the ground.

Hildur clutched at the tickets, smearing them in a shade of scarlet, gripping them tightly as they began to blur and distort through the building tears.

Shaking, she stood.

After taking what she needed from the others, she left them where they lay, and took Hans.

She carried him a short distance and sat them both down, at a larger opening in the earth, covered by moss, her arms clutched around him.

Moss: the concealer of damage and destruction at a volcanic level, covering it in something beautiful. If it could hide that, maybe it could hide Hildur's hurt?

She sat a while, embracing him and his company for the final time.

After this, she was on her own.

She took a few deep breaths, indulged a final thought, and then let go.

She watched him roll down the crevice, disappearing beneath the age-old lava, down below the ground, and eventually out of sight.

She stared into the darkness below.

A numbness overtook her, and she sat staring into nothingness; no longer thinking anymore, just...being.

The only thing that came to her were the words she had spoken to him earlier, but she didn't want to relive them, not now.

She willed the words not to replay themselves, but they didn't listen, and played anyway.

"Be careful... or the land will take you."

41

We Don't Fail

It wasn't until Hildur turned back onto the main road leading to the town that she realised she wasn't breathing properly.

Not enough to think straight anyway.

She consciously forced the breaths deeper, and slower. It felt robotic, but it began to work. The steering wheel seemed strange to turn, she realised she was gripping it so tightly that it made the turning erratic.

She eased off.

Hildur regained control, both of herself and the car.

Her eyes flicked between the road and the clock.

Just under ten minutes until departure.

She looked at the tickets.

The clock.

Then the road.

A flash of light in the rear view mirror from a distant car, fast coming down the mountain road, soon to be on the main stretch.

Maybe *them.*

Probably *them.*

They seemed far, but only a few minutes away. Hildur increased her speed, and was soon on the edge of the town. Although looking straight ahead, she saw nothing except the image of the open ground where Hans had disappeared into: pure, dark abyss.

She stared straight into it, and it back at her.

Right through her.

She felt the emptiness of a matching void within.

A pedestrian stepped out onto the road in front of her, and Hildur thanked the deep part of her subconscious that was aware enough to slam the brakes on.

She received an ominous glare, and rightfully so.

She forced the breaths deeper again, and slower.

The disgruntled pedestrian passed, as Hildur continued on, and headed for the ferry terminal.

*

'Put ya fuckin' foot down!'

'I am! This piece of shit is slow man.'

'Whatever, jus' fuckin' floor it, we can't lose 'em. We're the last ones now. Time to shine.'

The driver increased the speed even more, as Jakob continued, 'Plus, he'll have our heads if we fuck this up like the others.'

Jakob gripped the dashboard with one hand, the other hand squeezing his phone in a nervous vice: None of their calls had been answered, after some seven attempts to three different numbers.

The worst was assumed.

The team of four headed out instantly to the coastal town on Jakob's command, down the only road in or out. The other two men in the car kept watch of passing cars, scanning faces.

For Hildur's, or any nervous looking drivers, maybe with something to hide.

They sped on into the town, slowing just enough to allow the car to make the first turn. After just two corners, the ferry was visible, smoke billowing to the sky.

Almost ready for departure.

Jakob leaned forwards, willing himself ever closer to it.

'Focus now boys, we don't fail like the others. This is where it ends!'

42

What I Am

Hildur ditched the car at the end of the road, and bustled her way past a smattering of pedestrians that were outside the town's cafe and restaurant.

She was halfway through passing, when she stopped dead in her tracks at a foreign sound, coming from her pocket.

Not the ringtone she was used to, but from the phone she had taken from Axel.

She knew who would be on the other end.

She took it out and stared at the screen, stared at his name.

Seeing it lit up and in her face brought back memories she didn't want to think of, so she got rid of them, and answered.

Two people who loved the silence did what they did best, until one of them unusually broke out from their characteristics, and flew into the offensive with expletives.

'How fucking dare you! More of my people? And Axel no less! How did you even—' he said as he cut himself off, 'no, you know what, don't answer that. I will just get it out of you when I see you, when I have you begging for me to—'

'Shut it, Ulrik,'

A stunned silence.

Nobody said his name, especially not like that. They were to follow orders only: Y*es Sir, no Sir; I'm sorry Sir, please give me another chance.*

He was still in shock, so Hildur took control.

'I don't care what you're gonna do. I know what you will do, you're predictable. I'm just one person, and I'm the best... was the best, that you had. You won't even see me coming.'

Ulrik kicked back into life.

'And how do you think this will go for Atli? Or for your father? If you don't think they won't suffer consequences for what you've done, then you're wrong.'

Hildur looked up at the sudden mechanical noise: the ferry ramp lifting, signifying the end of cars docking – and soon, passengers.

Time to move.

'It's only thanks to your father that you got to be where you are, and to me for allowing it. We made you. *I* made you!'

Annoying as it was, Hildur couldn't deny that one.

So she embraced it instead.

'Yeah, that may be true.'

Ulrik scoffed at the admission.

'Both of you may have made me what I am today; but I will choose what I want to be tomorrow.'

Ulrik snapped again.

'YOU! YOU THINK YOU CAN JUST FUCKI—'

The rage grew – with all the words under the sun making their way out of the speaker in rapid fire – as two passing tourists stopped and stared in shock at the screeching phone that lay on the bench outside the cafe.

With no apparent owner, they looked around to search for one.

In the distance, they saw a woman walking away, hands in pockets, as calm as the setting sun itself.

150

43

Time To Leave

She couldn't help but turn to look; to see if they had arrived yet.

But nothing.

Not yet, anyway.

She turned back, took a step forward, and stopped as she heard it.

Tyres screeching.

The noise echoed and bounced around, signifying it was just a few roads away.

She picked up the pace in her walk as well as in her mind, running through last minute ideas and alternatives.

Tyres spliced through the thought as they screeched again, louder, the sound more direct.

One road away.

She was out of choices now. She had to board.

There was nowhere left to run, they had been driven to the edge of the land.

And under it.

It was time to leave

After boarding, the elderly man showed her the way, and took her to the bow of the vessel.

Hildur stood still, looking outward, not daring to glance back anymore.

Whatever happened from now on was out of her control. She had done all she could.

No more fighting.

She heard the anchors being released, the ship starting to budge, and the rumble of the engine increasing.

Freedom, seconds away.

*

After identifying the abandoned vehicle in the car park as their own rental, they did likewise and boarded their ferry.

The four men made it past the gate, despite the protests of a somewhat slack ticket guard. They were two minutes over boarding time, but four stern glares had made the employee think twice about enforcing the rule, and let them on.

If only he knew.

They split into two groups, and advanced through the ship, scanning all passengers for their target. A few uneasy eyes looked on as they pulled their children closer to them.

The hull took the longest, holding a hundred or more people, but still no sign. They swept through at a pace, four pairs of eyes sweeping left to right, clocking every face, every detail.

Trained and skilled eyes, four metal detectors, searching for their prize in the sand.

It was only a matter of time.

They always got their prize.

Having found nothing, they came to the end – the bow of the ship – one of the teams arriving just before the other.

Jakob signalled to the other couple to stay back as he approached with the remaining henchman at his side, both with hands on their holsters at the ready.

Some unsettled passengers began to scurry out of the way at the sight of weapons, and Jakob gestured for them to move back, clearing a path to the figure at the front. They all had eyes fixed on the solitary woman standing in the apex of the handrail, hood up, concealed. Just a small jut of blonde hair protruded outwards. Hands in pockets.

Still.

Passive.

The team glanced around at one another, sharing a smile along with a similar thought.

She knew she was outnumbered and wouldn't stand a chance.

She had given up.

The ship jolted and started to pull away. They were on the way; and she was trapped.

They had their target, at long last.

Jakob reached out, positioned his hand over her shoulder, and grabbed her.

44

They Both Knew

As soon as she felt the hand on her shoulder, Hildur spun around.

That warm smile.

Those piercing blue eyes.

She couldn't help but smile back at him. After all, the old man had been extremely kind.

His warm expression put her at ease, for the first time in hours.

'It'll be windy on the way; you'll need more than that. I'll get you an extra coat.'

Hildur's smile became fully-formed now. 'Thank you.'

The man disappeared into the compact cabin, and brought back a hefty parka to help keep the wind at bay.

Hildur looked across to the vast ferry, which was also on its way now.

Their little boat paled in comparison to the mammoth vessel.

She noticed a small gathering at the front of the ferry, what looked to be like several men, all above average build and height, and wearing dark clothes. Two of them were animated, waving their arms in the air. An argument maybe, they were certainly displeased. A main aggressor seemed to do most of the shouting.

Jakob.

A small figure stood by them, looking uncomfortable and diminutive, before running away.

Hildur couldn't help but wonder what she would have done if she was that smaller figure, if she had gotten trapped on there.

Fight, or give in?

Although it could have turned out differently, and Hans hadn't made it out, at least she had. She allowed herself to enjoy that small part, and to see them flail about in anger and confusion, before turning back to the front to face the horizon.

The mountains on both sides subsided as they sailed out of the bay, and soon there was nothing around them except for the open expanse of ocean.

It would be some five hours before they would arrive in the Faroe Islands, giving Hildur a much needed break and time to plan, but probably a little bit too much time to think.

She wanted to get to the land as quickly as possible and get away from all this, make a plan, and then disappear.

She would still need to get off at the next island, and hope they wouldn't discover that she was there. But she had to plan for that scenario.

She had to be ready for anything.

She put the planning to one side, and just enjoyed the view.

The sight of freedom, fast approaching.

She allowed her shoulders to be at ease, as well as her mind. No more scanning for threats. Her breaths were no longer laboured and shallow, they flowed deeply, in and out, in rhythm with the waves lapping against the side of the boat.

As she settled in the stillness, her mind awoke, and she felt it pull at her again, the decision that had been the catalyst for all of this. She hadn't had time to relive all of it, not until now.

The memory was faint and hazy, especially in contrast to the burning brightness of the evening's almost-sunset. But it was still there, clinging on in the back of her mind.

She couldn't take her eyes off of it... Hildur glared at her, eyes and syringe at the ready, about to put an end to her target. The woman was frozen, and then her hand lowered, and rested on her stomach; an uneven stroke, making its way over the protruding bump. She straightened her back upright, grunting at the effort of lifting several months of growth at the front. Her plea was now so hushed it was almost inaudible, "Please..."

Hildur closed her eyes, and lowered the syringe. She was reduced physically now, no more in a readied state. A part of her tried to lift her arm to strike – her practical side. But nothing moved. Another, stronger part of her stopped it from happening. The inward conflict resulted in her arm trembling at her side, shaking in indecision. Hildur never thought she would come here for this. She had prepared to fight for years, just not with herself. This was an entirely different opponent.

The woman slid past Hildur, hesitantly, staying square-on to her to not show her back, and keeping her eyes on her the whole time. She didn't blink once. Hildur remained completely still, and then the woman was past. She made for the door, turning towards it the closer she got with each step.

With one last glance back at her almost-killer, she whispered, "Thank you," and was out of the door, and lost to the night.

Hildur remained still in the silence, alone in the room, with nothing but her thoughts.

She opened her eyes, and despite the blinding light bouncing off the water, she saw things clearer than she had in a long time.

That decision had led to several deaths, including Hans', and flipping TESS upside down and into turmoil. She wondered if she would make the same choice again, given the chance.

She thought about it for about a second, and then stopped. She knew the answer.

There were no more feelings of unease, no nerves, and no doubts.

Only complete contentment.

She looked back to Iceland one last time, taking in its mountainous fjords and paint-pallet skyline. A place that had been a home to her as a child, and again for the past few days. Returning as a stranger, remembering, and now leaving feeling connected once more.

A realisation flowed over her.

She would return again.

As they finished exiting the harbour, and were about to be out in amongst the expanse, the elderly man caught her eye, smiled, and said, 'It's time.'

Hildur smiled.

Of course it is.

She thought of Hans once more, and turned back to face her next destination.

The waves ceased splashing against the sides as they became at ease with themselves, and all around them.

The ocean was at complete rest; one still entity.

Hildur closed her eyes, and became the very same.

The sun was low on the horizon now, and, as usual, threatened to set. But they both knew that it wouldn't.

Can I Ask You A Favour?

If you enjoyed this book, I´d really appreciate it if you could spare a few seconds to leave a short review.
Reviews are really important for new indie books such as this one, they go a long way to help.
I read all of them myself, and love hearing your feedback.

Please leave a review on:
Amazon
Goodreads

Thank you for your support!

About the Author

Hailing from both Berkshire and Dorset in the UK, and having spent a few years living and coaching football in Greece, Israel, and the Philippines, Matt is now settled and resides in Reykjavik, Iceland.

In between coaching Icelandic youth football and throwing axes, Matt writes fiction in his spare time, to help pass through the cold winter months.

Follow him on:
Twitter/Insta/Facebook: @MJFurtek

Website: https://mjfurtek.com/ - Sign up to the newsletter to receive early news and unique content.
Email: info@mjfurtek.com

Acknowledgements

It wouldn't be fair to release this without giving special thanks to the people who helped make this happen, both directly and indirectly.

So, in no order of importance, they are:

Jamie, for all the early video calls during lockdown, when this all began.

David and Anna, for proofreading and keeping my punctuation in check.

Dad and Ivana, for creating a cracking cover.

Mum, for offering help with just about everything along the way.

Ivana, again, for helping and pushing me on a daily basis with everything for the last year.

To everyone who read the book and offered feedback before publication.

And last of all to Iceland itself, for its inspiring scenery and calmness.

Printed in Great Britain
by Amazon

82416713R00098